ROSAMOND L...

was born in Buckinghamshire... the four children of R. C. Leh....... .... Beatrix Lehmann, the actress; her brother is the writer John Lehmann. She was educated privately and was a scholar at Girton College, Cambridge. She wrote her first novel, *Dusty Answer*, in her early twenties. In 1928 she married the Honourable Wogan Philipps, the artist, with whom she had one son and one daughter. In 1930 her second novel, *A Note in Music*, appeared. *Invitation to the Waltz* followed in 1932 and its sequel *The Weather in the Streets* in 1936. During the war she contributed short stories to *New Writing* which was edited by her brother: these were published as *The Gipsy's Baby* in 1946. *The Ballad and the Source* was published in 1944 followed in 1953 by *The Echoing Grove* which was to be her last novel for many years. *A Sea-Grape Tree*, the novel she published twenty-three years later in 1976, took up characters and themes from both *The Gipsy's Baby* and *The Ballad and the Source*, themes also echoed in her partial autobiography *The Swan in the Evening* (1967).

Rosamond Lehmann is one of the most distinguished British novelists of this century. An International Vice-President of International PEN, Vice-President of the College of Psychic Studies and a member of the Council of the Society of Authors, she has five grandchildren and lives in London and in Suffolk, near Aldeburgh. Virago publishes *Invitation to the Waltz*, *The Weather in the Streets*, *A Note in Music*, *The Gipsy's Baby*, *The Ballad and the Source*, *A Sea-Grape Tree* and *The Swan in the Evening*.

If you would like to know more about Virago books, write to us at Ely House, 37 Dover Street, London W1X 4HS for a full catalogue.

Please send a stamped addressed envelope

VIRAGO
Advisory Group

Book Tokens

Give them the pleasure of choosing

Book Tokens can be bought and exchanged at most bookshops.

THE SWAN
IN THE EVENING

Fragments of an Inner Life

ROSAMOND LEHMANN

Revised and with a new epilogue by
the author

Published by VIRAGO PRESS Limited 1982
Ely House, 37 Dover Street, London W1X 4HS

First published by Willam Collins Ltd 1967

Virago edition offset from Collins 1977 edition

British Library Cataloguing in Publication Data
Lehmann, Rosamond
    The swan in the evening.—Rev. ed.
    1. Lehmann, Rosamond—Biography
    I. Title
    823'.912   PR6023.E42Z/
                ISBN 0-86068-299-4

Printed in Great Britain by litho
at The Anchor Press, Tiptree, Essex

DEDICATED TO

Anna

MY ELDEST GRANDCHILD

ACKNOWLEDGEMENTS

The author is grateful for permission to quote the lines from 'Little Gidding' and 'Burnt Norton' by T. S. Eliot published in *Four Quartets* by Messrs Faber and Faber Ltd; to James Mac-Gibbon for permission to quote from the unpublished letter from Stevie Smith, from her review of *The Swan in the Evening* first published in the *Listener* and from her poem 'Oh Christianity, Christianity' published in *The Collected Poems* by Allen Lane, and in *Me Again: The Uncollected Writings of Stevie Smith* published by Virago Press; and to Sir Rupert Hart-Davis for permission to quote from the unpublished letter from William Plomer.

LIST OF ILLUSTRATIONS

All the photographs in this book reproduced by kind permission of Rosamond Lehmann.

PART ONE

'Go said the bird, for the leaves were
full of children,
Hidden excitedly, containing laughter.
Go, go, go, said the bird: human kind
Cannot bear very much reality.'

Burnt Norton, Four Quartets, T. S. Eliot

1

I was born during a violent thunderstorm; and since the date was the third day of February, this disturbance of the elements struck the popular imagination with dramatic force, as being, in the strict sense of the word, phenomenal. Nobody, I hasten to add, related the portent to my personal entry into the twentieth century A.D. The time was not long after 1 a.m. of the day of the funeral of Queen Victoria. It was only myself, as I started to emerge from the animal-vegetable swaddlings of infancy, whom the coincidence impressed. It seemed to give me an unexpectedly distinguished *cachet*: almost the reflection of a royal nimbus.

One day, around the age of five, sitting in my kindergarten class with a tray before me of soft white sand in which letters of the alphabet are to be traced, I call out suddenly to Miss Davis and confide in her what a notable birthday is mine.

'Very interesting dear; but pay attention now, please.' Pretty Miss Davis, whom I adore, to whom I have publicly, gratuitously offered my passport, lays it down, patiently, as an irrelevance, thereby obliterating whatever it was that had seemed all at once to startle the dark backward of my identity with such a flash. Now I feel pinched in my chest because the other children stare at me; their cold eyes make a nothing of me, a WRONG SUM AGAIN. . . . Rub her out, cry baby cry . . .

Yet a few months later a similar urge wells up and over-masters me. This time it is in drill. March, march, round and round the schoolroom to a rollicking tune from Miss Davis at the piano. *Halt!* The music breaks off. I call out: 'Miss Davis!' on a reckless note.

'Yes, what is it?'

'I don't like being in the middle.'

'What do you mean, dear?' Puzzle for Miss Davis. I have in fact been top of the class this week and in consequence I lead the march.

'Well . . . I'm not the oldest . . . and I'm not the youngest. . . .' Now I have qualms. 'Helen's older and Baby (my sister Beatrix) is —'

'Ah yes, I see.' She breaks into a soft chuckle. 'Well, I'm the middle one too, in my family. I think it's rather nice. Like the jam in the middle of a sandwich. Attention children, forward *march*! Heads up! Swing your arms!'

Forward I march, leading a Band of Hope, to the tune of *John Brown's Body*. When it comes to *glory glory Allelujah!* we belt it out with a will, I loudest of all for once, and most rejoicing. For lo! I am absolutely on the map, the sweet surprise of it! – I am linked with Miss Davis, middle one of the family, I am the jam between the bread slices, given status and protection.

Miss Winifred Davis is tall, willowy and pale, with liquid, faintly protuberant eyes of violet flecked with

10

green, and a cloud of ash-blonde hair. Her voice is low
and caressing. Soon she will vanish from our lives. One
day we break up for the summer holidays – always a day
of sportive leaps and chatter; we kiss her good-bye until
next term; and unaccountably she is not clasping us to
her full-bloused breast (smocked tussore) with smiles and
jokes, but speechless and raining tears.

'Why is Miss Davis crying?'

'Don't you *know*? *I* know!'

She is going to be married. Doesn't she want to be?
Yes, she does want to be. Then why . . .? She will be
Mrs. Tinkler. At this we burst into hilarious shrieks: we
bandy the name about, competing in flights of wit. But
perhaps she weeps because she doesn't like her new funny
name; and now I have sympathetic qualms, and try to
choke back my laughter. I see that hers is a natural
distress, for the funniness inherent in the syllables casts
an unsuitably derogatory spell upon her, and upon our
relations with her, and her tears seem to say that she is
being down-scrambled by our mockery, doesn't like it,
cannot help it. It is a shame.

We are assembled on the porch of our school, namely
the brick and stucco pavilion built by our parents in the
garden to house our education; and all of a sudden from
nowhere, Mr. Tinkler materializes. He stands beside
Miss Davis, immensely tall, thin, dark, with flashing
spectacles. His arm is linked in hers; she is beaming,
blushing, mopping her eyes. He has come to fetch her
away, fetch her away. . . . Some nurse or parent present

to collect her charge calls out officiously: 'Three cheers for the bride and bridegroom! Hip, hip!' – and feebly we pipe: 'Hurrah!'

But won't she be coming back? No, of course not, says someone heartily. She is going to live in Birmingham, and have lots of children of her own to look after. Then, shall I never see her again? . . .

The question is unasked, unanswered. Strange, strange to relate, I did see her once again, many years later; but I don't think – I shall never be sure if – she saw me. I am in my twenties, the author of *Dusty Answer* and quite often photographed. I am lunching alone in my London Club, and my eye is caught by two figures at a far table in the opposite corner; an attractive fair fresh-faced young man, and a thin faded-looking lady in black. Presently this young man gets up, comes towards me, and addresses me with a mixture of shyness and easy charm. 'Might I be Rosamond Lehmann?

'I thought I recognized you,' he says. 'My mother cut out your photograph. . . . She was always so interested. . . . She taught you once. The name is Tinkler.'

He is pleased that I respond so eagerly and remember so vividly, but the conversation proceeds with growing awkwardness. I follow his uncertain glance over his shoulder. Can it be —? She is not looking at me or at him but fixedly ahead of her. She has two flaming patches on her thin cheek-bones and gives an impression of tremulous disarray. 'Yes, that is my mother,' says this charming young man. 'I'm afraid she isn't at all well just at present. My father died suddenly in the spring and it shook her terribly. She had a breakdown. But I hope,' he added, resolutely cheerful, 'she's over the worst.'

Was he asking me to come and speak to her? – or delicately explaining that it would be wiser not to? I shall never know; and must for ever accuse myself of cowardly failure to find out.

I charge him with my love to her; he is to say I have never forgotten her kindness to me, and her beauty. He nods thanks and returns to his own table.

I steal one look before I hurry from the room and from the building. Dislocation, preoccupation are evident; a couple precariously tethered to their situation. The pathos of filial stiff upper lip strikes me forcibly.

Her dual image shocks, compels my imagination many days: the recollected one, *allegra*, in its silvery nimbus; this one *dolorosa*, lustreless; the discrepancy between the young and the older image is bridged by the tears of both.

Dearest Miss Davis, you were too vulnerable. Never more did a figure remotely resembling yours shine in the interminable, sometimes glum and eccentric path of my educational years. Quite soon after, I was learning to play the piano with Mademoiselle's gold watch placed alternately on the back of the left hand and the right, to maintain the correct flat position. When the watch slipped off she caught it and smacked my hand with a ruler. Quite soon, instead of being comforted when I fell down and cut my knees, I was being put to bed as a punishment for tearing my stockings.

.

2

Further back, further than the white sands of kindergarten lies my first conscious memory: so far back that it is much less visual than tactile. A dark obstacle, perhaps a wall or a door, obstructs me; I pat on its polished surface and hear the thump of my hand. I look up, and it is a little house with a window too high for me to look through. Suddenly the door of the little house opens with a squawk; I am swooped down on, snatched up, clasped in hard arms, pressed against black sour-smelling cloth, amid the glint and rattle of buttons, brooches, dentures, watch-chains. A cheek is pressed to mine – female, I recognize, but *hairy*; at the same time a succession of high-pitched crooning endearments assaults my ear. I yell and yell for rescue; and presumably rescue comes; for that is all that I remember.

But later this experience, together with the background and the protagonists, is verified. The place was St. Pierre en Port, my age was eighteen months; the little house of dark polished wood was the enclosed reception desk wherein sat Mademoiselle Sidonie, sister of the proprietor of our hotel, spinster, child-lover, and – poor afflicted lady – bristlingly moustached.

She went on sending us postcards from Guernsey for a long time afterwards; and I have a faint recollection of being told how unmerited was my generous portion of this kind attention. One of the postcards has stuck in my memory: a ginger tom cat in striped bathing drawers extending his paws and claws with a disquieting grin. Across him, written in a flowing French hand: *Le chat dit Bonjour à la petite Rose! ! !*

3

Early memories have, I suppose, something inevitably traumatic in their composition. They record moments of being shocked, pitchforked out of the dream of wake which is our natural infant state: shocked out to register the pain of the first lesions in the adhesive web which our senses spin for the protection of our untempered bodies.

For instance: an enormous Teddy bear wearing a clown's hat and a red, blue, green and yellow harlequin suit lies on his back upon the nursery floor. Abandoned to delirious mirth and unco-ordinated gymnastics we go on jumping on to his stomach to hear him growl. Myself and Baby: he is as tall as she. All at once a cascade of blood obliterates her flushed, wild face. There is no sound from her (she does not see what I see) but I let out scream upon scream; and someone comes rushing, exclaims, whips her up and disappears with her. I follow, and beat on the bathroom door, wailing that it is my fault, my fault. Presently she is carried back, washed, clean, on the pale side but composed, laid flat on the nursery sofa and told in the charged, scolding voice special to parents and nurses who have had a 'turn', to mind and stop acting silly for a change. A murmurous discussion ensues, between Lizzie our nurse and our nursemaid Lucy – beautiful Lizzie and rose-cheeked Lucy, soon to get married and abandon us like most of the pleasant faces and good-tempered voices that spread an Eden, early lost, around our nursery days. 'Funny thing to happen. . . . Shall you mention it?' . . . 'I may do.' 'Must have burst a blood vessel. . . .' 'What did the other say it was her fault for?' . . . 'You may well ask. She never touched her. . . .' 'Then why is she creating?'

Why indeed? Except that when it appears, even a few drops of it, blood, sacrificial, streams in the whole firmament of childhood.

Once again I have made an exhibition of myself and it is better to ignore me.

And yet again: My mother takes me, in the Victoria, to somebody's birthday party at Cookham. (Why only me? But so it is.) On the sunny lawn are assembled about two dozen little girls and boys whom I have never seen before. We are lined up, given wooden spoons with plaster eggs in them. Ready, steady, GO! 'Run, run, don't drop, pick up your egg, run, steady now, well done Eric, Eric's won, who's next? Norah, well done Norah. . . . Brenda third. . . . Who comes in last, eggless, and in tears? 'Bad luck Rosie, never mind dear. . . .' Where is my mother? Vanished indoors. What is this abomination of desolation called SPORTS?

The cruel children fly all over the lawn, casual and

sharp as birds. They compete and compete, as if competing was the height of fun. They jump over obstacles and crawl under them and climb up and down them; they tie their inside legs together with handkerchiefs and run in couples. I conceal myself appropriately beneath a weeping willow and watch, despairing, from a distance. A kind lady comes to coax me out: I will not come.

My state is such that when my mother comes at last with an unpleased face to lead me to the tea-table she murmurs: 'Take no notice of her'; and nobody does. Not one of those cheerful girls and boys takes the slightest notice of the hiccuping sodden object in their midst.

Now comes prize giving. Prizes, prizes, prizes, every sort and kind, are displayed upon a trestle table on the lawn. At once my eye is caught by a small round-bodied scent bottle, green glass overlaid with silver fretwork, and with a lovely stopper like an emerald jujube. It looks a bit lost among the other prizes, as if it had been taken off somebody's dressing-table at the last moment, just in case of a miscalculation. I covet it unspeakably. Every boy or girl who has won a race is called up in turn to choose a prize. Next, the also rans – not to choose, but to be given something. Nobody will go home empty-handed. The table is getting barer. *The scent bottle remains.*

'Oh, Rosie!' Our hostess looks at me dubiously, then at the table, stripped now of every single object except – 'You must have a consolation prize. What about this little scent bottle?'

The joy is piercing. How can it be that this treasure has fallen into no other hands but mine? How is it that, at the last moment, I have become the luckiest girl at the party?

On the drive home, I remark happily:

'It's just exactly the one thing I wanted!'

'You didn't deserve it,' replied my mother, justly pointing to the frightful abyss between my merits and my expectations. I clasp my consolation prize, but it feels cold now, tarnished. No question of it: I hold between my palms extravagant dishonour and reward.

And yet again: I am holding to the nose of my infant brother a flask of eau-de-Cologne (curious that the perfume *motif* should thus recur): He seizes it, tilts it, and at one gulp swigs down a fair portion of its contents. I stare. He stares back. Can all be well with him? All is not well. A second later a muffled choking roar announces his inner consternation. Julia his nurse appears. I bleat: 'He *drank* it. I meant him just to smell it.' Her face turns pale as junket, and his is now dark plum colour. As she charges from the room with him she flings across her shoulder:

'You may have been the death of him.'

Well, I have been the death of him. I hurry away and creep under my bed, and there, in my best cotton frock, entomb myself, inhaling the peppery smell of carpet and carpet dust, and listening as from the world of shades to far-off voices interspersed with dreadful silences. I am due to go to Henley Regatta – prime treat of the year;

but they can call and call, I will never come out. Presently the vibration of the car rises, diminishes, and fades along the drive. My father is headed for the Umpire's Launch; he cannot brook delay. But can my mother and Helen really have accompanied him, indifferent to or unaware of the fatality? I practise saying sincerely to my parents: 'It was an accident.' The memory of Boy's congested outraged face is lacerating. 'You gave me poison to drink,' it says, *'on purpose.'*

The silence now seems absolute. Perhaps Julia has charged with him to Nanny Green, her friend, expert in croup and other mysteries, who lives near by . . . or to the doctor . . . or the undertaker. . . .

Time passes. Then I hear sounds impossible to associate with domestic tragedy. Shrieks and peals, with deep gardeners' voices interspersed. The maids are in splits in the kitchen, at their elevenses: a not uncommon occurrence whenever their employers are abroad. The day is not doom-laden, but ordinary. The call of nature obliges me to emerge. I gaze from the bathroom window and see my brother setting forth as usual in his pram, with Julia at the helm. He looks his customary outdoor self – an infant version of Mithras, Sun God, rayed round by the layers of a *broderie anglaise* sun hat, tied in a dashing bow beneath his chins. I hurry down to join them in the garden. He is unequivocally pleased to see me, and seems devoid of rancour or of mortal symptoms. 'Wherever have you been?' exclaims Julia sharply, eyeing me. 'They had to go without you.' I am silent, sheepish. She does not demur when I grip the handle of the pram and start to push. 'I told your mother,' she says presently, 'you felt a wee bit sicky after breakfast. It might be as well for you to stay here quiet with Birdie Boy and me.' I remain dumb. 'And who's his favourite sis-sis?' she cries, addressing her impassive charge.

She too is sheepish, I realize; also she has not given me away; also she is sorry for what she said; also has been agitated by my disappearance. But to refer to or admit to even one facet of this complex would be *infra dig*.

4

No grown-up, in my personal experience, ever said sorry to a child in those days. None, in the event of inability to answer a question, ever confessed to simple ignorance. As for subjects such as birth, death, physical and sexual functions, these were taboo, and invested with an aura of murk, shame, guilt, suggestiveness and secrecy. Children today are more likely to be spared taboos, whatever strains and stresses have been substituted. In some aspects of our sheltered, materially privileged childhood, my sisters and I happened to be unlucky. There was a period when, at least as regards our schoolroom life, and certainly whenever our parents were away, we took a considerable bashing; when there was no knowing when – or why – nemesis would overtake us. Perhaps I came off lightest, being too much of a coward not to try to court approval. But a part of one sister's whole life has been coloured, I think, by the burning sense of injustice kindled at that time; and as for the other, it seems to me that it took her many years and all her strength of character to resolve the blocks, mental and emotional, engendered by unlove in the nursery.

By contrast, 'outdoors' remained idyllic, numinous, the gardeners loved, trusted, admired for their skills, their smell of earth and potting shed, the sense of reliability, simplicity, goodness of heart they emanated. And in the servants' hall was perpetual kindliness, willingness to listen, exclaim, explode with laughter, declare that we were cautions, cough-drops; there was carolling out of *After the Ball was Over*, the *Mistletoe Bough, Daisy*, and other popular ditties. At times, during parental absences and the consequent supremacy of Mademoiselle, and *punitions* our daily lot, when their charged expressions clearly said it was a crying shame. So, I thought, did the big dogs.

Goodman, Godden, Bob Field, Stacey; Seymour, Edith, Ethel, Rhoda Annie, Sarah, Mabel, Nellie, Cloudie, Mrs. Almond – thank you with all my heart. . . . There is also James in the pantry to be affectionately remembered: James with his huge blank bald face like a Thurber drawing, and those fingers like bunches of mauve bananas which he employs of an afternoon in the tatting of yards upon yards of lace. He sits in a deck-chair in the pantry, a little shawl across his shoulders, amid thick exhalations of plate-polish, his frock-coat hung on a peg behind the door; James who started life as an infant prodigy trombone player, who later abandoned show business, and after a lifetime of service with my grandparents and my parents, and after quarrelling with a succession of unsatisfactory (but to me glamorous) young footmen, found his ideal adopted son in one Ernest Brimblecombe and retired to end his days with him.

There is also unforgettable Mrs. Slezina, 'Dickie', tiny black antique fairy, almost a midget, in the sewing-room: Dickie whose portrait I drew as Tilly in *The Ballad and The Source*. Her room smells of camphor and liquorice, and sometimes she consents to dance for us when we visit her to hear her talk about our grandmother or to watch the cuckoo clock when the hours strike. On one wall of her attic room is a small, very strange picture to find there – or anywhere in our house. Against a blood-red and blue and orange sky a half-nude figure draped in crimson is standing in what seems to be a desert, with brown stick-like arms extended. Underneath this picture is written: OM MANI PADME HUM. The Sunrise Comes. Dickie doesn't know the meaning of it, but says it is a nice cheerful bit of colour. Sometimes as I mooch around the garden by myself I chant these words.

Above all, let me conjure William Moody in the stables: Moody from the Shetland Isles, coachman first, then chauffeur; sanguine of complexion, with noble features and hot blue eyes; a melancholy man of passions, whom his name suited well; whose sexual magnetism I was aware of at the age of four.

Once as I drive beside him on the box of the high dog cart with Yankee the big chestnut between the shafts, he tells me what a dentist is. 'A dentist is a man who airrns his daily brread from the cries of strong men, the moans of weak women, and the shrieks of little tenderr children.'

He had grievances and brooded over them. Once and once only he had taken Mrs. Moody to the Kent coast for a holiday. At the conclusion of this week, he was requested by his landlady to write a few words in her Visitors' Book, and he composed the following:

> *This boarding house, named Kidderpore,*
>   *Was advertised to be*
> *A home from home – and what is more*
>   *One minute from the sea.*
>
> *But as we tramp, as tramp we must,*
>   *Each morning to the shore*
> *We wonder why they made it just*
>   *One minute and no more.*
>
> *For no one in so short time could*
>   *Have* EVER *gone so far*
> *Unless they had a very good*
>   *And rapid motor car.*

This composition, frequently rendered at my request, in his rich slow Highland voice with dramatic stressed vowels and rolling 'rs' still rings in my ears.

'But what did she say when she *read* it?'

'Ah! we'd hooked it before she got a peep of it!' he would say with savage satisfaction. 'I made sure of that! There!' I says to her at parting, 'if it didn't almost slip my mind! A few lines as requested, with my compliments. Confound the mean mealy-mouthed miserly old devil!' Then he would burst into a shout of laughter. 'Took me two days and two nights to get that out on paper shipshape. Never again! Oh, it was wrung from a soul in travail! But it was wurrth it.'

My father declared that Moody's poem had all the attributes of the best light verse, and more than once called upon me to recite it to amuse his friends. When I repeat to Moody my father's tribute such a sudden wine-dark flush incarnadines his face that I am startled.

His wife was a tall, dark, gaunt woman, shy, taciturn: they seemed to be a team not made to pull together. They had two sons to whom Moody seemed more or less indifferent, and a little girl, Wilma, who was his heart's treasure. She had eyes of intense blue, speaking eyes, under a bulging brow, a thatch of bright rough hair, carnation cheeks, and a low hoarse voice. Wherever he was at work – forking the straw in the loose boxes around the chestnut rumps of Yankee and Bruno, whistling and polishing in the harness-room, up the ladder in the hayloft – she tagged along behind him, fearless under the horses' hooves, pick-a-back on his broad shoulders as he climbed the ladder or descended from it, dragging the watering can after him when he gardened of an evening. She was phenomenally precocious, original, comical, primitive: a child of the Outer Isles, a poet's child. Later when I read *Pet Marjorie* it seemed that I was reading about Wilma. They must have been children of the same Ray I think, destined to glow on earth and vanish swiftly, leaving the air of morning stained with their vividness. All that I remember of her last days is that I was suddenly forbidden to visit that richly charged magnetic field, the stables: Wilma had something very bad, catching, called diphtheria. In vain, at her last gasp, a trachaeotomy was performed. She died of suffocation. She was six years old.

The tragedy shattered us one and all. Julia sobbed in the nursery, harrowing herself, us, the nurse-maid, with recollections of the times she'd called it a sin and a shame, the way Mr. Moody spoilt that child. . . . Could Wilma have been taken as a judgement? . . . When she returned from paying her last respects, she conjured before our eyes the picture of unimaginable Wilma in her little coffin, clasping a bunch of forget-me-nots. The worst was the sight of my father weeping in the library. The kind of child he fancied most was precisely Wilma's kind – a clown child, an original, an extrovert; and Wilma's remarks and ways had always doubled him up. Now suddenly she had become a little angel, no laughing matter. Later he told me that Moody had asked him to write something for her epitaph. I found in an anthology Herrick's lines beginning *Here a pretty Baby lies*; and he said yes, he wished we had found them sooner; but by that time he had composed his own poignant verses for her and they are engraved on the white marble of her headstone.

We were all severely shaken; but we all recovered; all but Moody. More than once have I heard it said that we are never given more to bear than we are able to bear. It is not true, in my experience. Some of us cannot bear what we are given. Moody was one of these. Of course, now that he was so stricken I avoided him; and when we did meet it was plain that he couldn't be bothered with me any more – or with anybody else. If I had a message from my mother to deliver he acknowledged it curtly, courteously; otherwise not a syllable passed his rigid lips. His eyes, dull blue marbles shot with red, glared at nothingness.

Only one more memory returns. Again I am sitting beside him on the box and being driven through the purlieus of Marlow on my way to a tea-party. It is a slummy street of poor low houses, and from the door of one of them a little girl runs out into the road, almost brushes the wheel, darts back again. She is a ragged child and very dirty and has no shoes or stockings (barefoot boys and girls could still be seen when I was a child). Presently Moody says in a stone voice: '*She'll* live. Nobody wants her but she'll live – grow up to be a — and one that has every care, that's the apple of your eye, that you'd lay down your life for gladly. . . .'

Silence again.

Try as I may, not another word or image rises. How, why, when did he leave? . . . with no good-byes? Where he went afterwards, what he did? A nagging impression persists that things went ill for him, and iller; that he took to sad consolations; that his poor wife went one way with her boys, and he another. . . . But all that area is clouded.

Whether or no he tried to believe that his bold bad pagan babe was safe in the arms of Jesus, gone before, I do not know. He did not seem to profit from whatever the Church offered him, as doubtless it did offer him, in the way of exhortation to say God's Will Be Done.

Often and often I tried to summon a credible image of Wilma in the Elysian Fields; but this presumably idyllic spot, full of lilies, harps, crowns and angels' wings, got itself mixed up in my imagination with the sinister reality of another, an earthly field called Cookham Meadow, whither we repaired each spring to pick cowslips and kingcups. This too should have been an idyllic expedition; but every year as I reached and unwillingly climbed the stile, a hideous *malaise* plucked at my solar plexus. Somewhere in that expanse of flat damp pasture, rinsed with unearthly green, were . . . yes? . . . no? . . . *yes! ! – cows*: and they would charge, and trample us, and impale the dogs upon their horns, and none of us would ever get home again.

I ran about and picked and picked into my basket, in constant, surreptitious, dread anticipation. A long way off, or in the middle distance, the cows moved purposefully, stood still and menacingly stared, gradually approached. . . . At last came the blessed moment when my father whistled to the busy dogs and called us homeward. How merrily then did I hent the stile-o! how stout-hearted my backward look; how rapturously did I inhale the mysterious sweet breath of my cowslips, enjoy the green-gold lustre of my kingcups. We crossed the quiet road (no need in those days to shoot frenzied glances right and left before scurrying across) and flung ourselves against high wooden palings that bordered somebody's large garden. 'Lift me up, Daddy.' He lifted us in turn. 'Are the White Ladies there?' Yes, he can see them. I gaze, gaze, over lawn, flower-beds, pergolas, trellises, sanded paths, a tennis-court. '*I* see them!' But I never did. To this day I have no notion who, what were the White Ladies, how they had originated, whether my sisters were vouchsafed a sight of them, or whether, like myself, they pretended. My father was a born maker-up, and our part was to welcome his magical inventions and ceremoniously participate without asking questions. The White Ladies were good magic; so was Miss Echo who lived in the sky and called back to us, in her husky woodwind voice whatever we called when we came to a certain spot on Cockmarsh, under Winter Hill. But Cookham Meadow (which seemed to have disintegrated when I went last year to look for it) was tenanted, even without the cows, by some inimical or anyway heartless Presence – some brooding Deva. It was a place for watery spells and fairy rings and spectral mist-forms: Wilma would not care to play there with her new companions of the subtle regions.

Not till close on half a century later, when I in my
turn suffered the cruellest and seemingly most unnatural
of all human bereavements, did I think of her again, and
of her father, who must have joined her long ago;
remembering them as they had been together, in the
harness-room, the hayloft, the bit of garden, each the
other's innocent delight; then torn apart, stamped
upon, stamped out. . . . They then, I now: or so it seemed
in the first days after Sally left the earth. Yet at the same
time, on another mysterious level, it was as if they had
drawn close and were showing themselves to me in a way
I can only describe as 'living pictures'. I could not
account for this. Perhaps it was one of the hallucinations
I must expect, now that I had joined the age-long procession of broken-hearted mothers and fathers, like
Mr. and Mrs. Moody, and the parents of Marjorie Flem-
ing, and Mr. and Mrs. William Wordsworth and Mary and
Percy Bysshe Shelley, Patrick Brontë *père*, Monsieur du
Perrier, and William Shakespeare, and countless, countless others, illustrious, obscure, anonymous . . .

Now that I know that death considered as extinction
is an illusory concept based on the ignorance, or prejudice, or the intellectual arrogance or snobbery, or the
natural dread or not unnatural despair, or the built-in
death-wish – the *goût de cendre* – of blind humanity; and
that life goes on – relentlessly you might say, whether
or no we fancy the idea, and certainly in accordance with
cosmic laws which human reason is ill-equipped to understand; and certainly not in accordance with orthodox

Church creeds and dogmas: now that I know this for certain, it does not seem to me sentimental-fanciful, but possible, that within the eternally created and creating thought-web upon which are stamped our inter-connected dreams and destinations, those whom we seek with single-minded love we do find, or find again. And so, whether or not Wilma and her father 'came back', compassionately, to reassure me, there may well have been meaning in my seeing him, not in his old carapace of bitter blackness, when I identified him with that father in that poem of Kipling's:

> *For far, oh very far behind*
> *So far she cannot call to him*
> *Comes Tegumai, alone, to find*
> *The daughter that was all to him.*

but quietly showing himself, or shown to me, with Wilma by his side.

The last thing I intend is to set up dogmas of my own against the confirmed atheist, or the apostle of humanism or rationalism or any other kind of ism.

> *Reason has moons; but moons not hers*
> *Lie mirrored on her sea,*
> *Confounding her astronomers,*
> *But oh! – delighting me.*

If these lines of Ralph Hodgson, whose symbols and

imagery have haunted me since I was in my early teens, speak to me of reality and embody my own predilections, I hope I shall not be suspected of worshipping the dark gods of intuition and of mocking the paler gods of intellect. What I am writing is purely a personal testament, based upon experience; scrupulously recorded, and, I trust, consistent.

5

I am allotted one of the disused dog kennels set in the plantation of laurel and other shrubs that helps to screen the north side of my father's property from the smoke-belching engines that ever and anon draw into Bourne End station, halt, draw out again towards Cookham, or Wooburn Green, or Marlow, just beyond my range of vision. The trains are much loved by me; their language is companionable, familiar, pregnant with interest and surprises: triumphant masculine crescendos, gently lamenting diminuendos, hoarse throaty chucklings, indignant hoots, unbridled snorts and explosions, exhausted sighs and snuffles. Even the shunting goods trains are dear to me, especially in the dead of night, when their screech and cackle speak to me not of dementia but of hope and comfort: strong working men are awake out there, and doing manly things with brakes and lamps and signals: all must be well.

My kennel is one of three with high railings separating each from the next, and a concrete run between the outer and the inner wooden door. Here Rufus, spaniel saluted by my father in a celebrated dog poem, breathed his last after eighteen years and was laid to rest near by, in the Dogs' Cemetery, a sombre spot, whose engraved headstones commemorate the recurrent heart-breaks of our youth. I do not think that Helen ever occupied her kennel; that of Beatrix is austerely equipped, in a fashion befitting a Lone Scout. I furnish mine with an empty crate covered with pink gauze, a camp stool, a tin containing all the stale cake I can lay hands on, festoons of lilac and green shot chiffon (once waved and wafted by me in the Dance of the Wood Nymphs) across the entrance, a few chipped mugs and plates, and, in pride of place, on top of the crate, my aesthetic high spot: an ornamental vase depicting a cherub perched upon a gilt-edged receptacle scattered all over its outer surface with brilliantly purple pansies. Affixed to the walls by drawing-pins, ripped from a series entitled *Days with the Modern Masters*, hang certain of my favourite colour prints: The Blessed Damozel; Bubbles; and a lady called Hope, barefoot, powerfully built, classically draped in clinging blue, seated on an orange and drifting with bowed head and bandaged eyes through mists of a similar blue.

I decide to use my residence as a hospital for birds. These, chiefly blackbirds and thrushes, it is my mission to rescue from the strawberry nets and the raspberry nets during Goodman's lunch hour: for Goodman, despite his name, and his high-minded nature, has a ruthless, Mr. McGregor side to him. Sometimes it suffices to steal upon the agitated poachers, then quickly to raise the net, and out they dart and away with a cry which I interpret as 'thanks, good-bye'. But sometimes, wing-tangled, trapped by neck and claw, their plight is desperate. So is mine. With beating heart and hands that strive to overcome their clumsiness, I pinion them; my scissors feverishly snip and snip. When, sometimes, after their release, they stay quite still between my open palms, my breath stops. Have they fainted? Generally, when I put them down they start to revive, and after a moment hop or flap away; but now and then they keel over with their eyes shut, and then I bear them tenderly to hospital and place them on a bed of cotton wool inside my crate, with a saucer of bread and milk beside them; then creep away, raising the gauze *so that their mothers can come for them*. Whether or no something of this nature does occur, at all events, when I return a few hours later, or perhaps next morning, the hospital bed is empty. But one day I extricate a young blackbird caught by the neck. As soon as I cut him down his head sags; his wing is broken too. The case seems grave, so I wrap him up completely in cotton wool before placing him in the box and tiptoeing away. Then oblivion, based probably upon foreboding, supervenes. Days pass before my next visit to the kennel. The ball of cotton wool lies as I left it, motionless . . . no, not absolutely motionless. . . . There

seems a sort of pervasive stir or tremor. . . . I open it;
drop it, aghast; take to my heels.

After that, my house stands vacant in perpetuity.
Long afterwards I venture to look in. Someone has taken
away my beautiful pansy vase; also that cotton wool;
also *Bubbles*; but *Hope* and *The Damozel* are still there,
discoloured, presiding over shreds of damp gauze and
chiffon.

Perhaps my propensity for more immaterial dwellings
stems from that traumatic moment. Now I have houses
all over the garden: in the fork of the walnut tree, where
I write poetry, in the rock-garden, where I queen it as
Amaranth Aurora and send forth my Attendant Fairy,
Starstripe, to do my magic biddings; round the lily
pond where I watch the goldfish and catch tadpoles
and frog-spawn in jam-jars; under the green-gold,
dark-ribbed skirts of the weeping beech; in the apple
orchard where I thrust the creaking swing to dizzy
glimpses over the garden wall; in jungles of syringa, lilac,
berberis, japonica, through which I crawl and tear my
stockings and snarl up my long hair; at one end or the
other of the herbaceous border where I simply crouch,
motionless, hidden so I imagine, in thickets of obliterating
leaf, sun-soaked or rain-drenched, studded and spangled
with the fire-blue, fire-rose, tawny, lemon, crystal-white
and green of buds and petals; breathing in their aromatic
exhalations. In those days, borders danced with butter-
flies, not only the frolic whites among the lavender, but
tortoise-shells, peacocks, chalk-blues, cloudy yellows –

even the rare red admiral and swallowtail. The dreaming sentience of the plant world entered into me; its gossamer awareness enmeshed me. Did I ever see nature spirits? I never doubted their reality and presence; or that we communicated without words. It was safer to be in love with flowers than with birds, dogs, kittens, donkeys, tortoises. The dangers and responsibilities were less by a long chalk; and when they died, nothing awful happened: they withered, vanished, came again; whereas I knew now what death was for animals: it was the worm made visible. My murmured 'Sorry!' to each flower I picked or broke off by mistake was somewhat automatic. They didn't feel it, of course they couldn't feel, of course, of course. . . . However, just in case they did, I had magic words to stop the pain and ward off their reproaches.

6

Sometimes the power of words got out of hand and turned on me.

I am in the Parish Hall; it is a Sale of Work. I circulate among the visitors with a trayful of lavender bags which I proffer to a long lean sallow nurse in a grey uniform. I know her: she looks after a little boy with a squint and a funny way of talking, who is said to have tantrums and beat his head against his nursery wall, who once presented me with a letter that said, in grimy reeling print: 'Dear Rosy sprinkel me with kisses if you want my luv to gro yore everlasting Joey.' This nurse bends down to me, smiling, and says in a low confidential voice: '*I'm stony broke.*' At once such terror grips me that I almost swoon. Why? How was it that this harmless if unfamiliar slang phrase took sinister form as she uttered it and dropped on me with the chill weight of granite? Absurd, morbid child. . . . Mad, like all children . . .: or so very little madder.

Yet could there be perhaps, in each one of us, a residue of consciousness, deeper than human, deeper than animal, bird, fish, reptile, plant: a residue within which such petrifying similes and symbols might reflect some primordial stage of evolution? Might a mineral ache be still imprisoned in us, struggling to thrust the first shudder of prescience, perturbation, over the threshold of inertia? . . . However that may be, there are days when echo answers *stony broke* if our souls call the question; when to dig down is to expose a site strewn with dried-up objects whose meaning, if any, seems at once too loaded and too hollow to be borne. Thrones, tombs, bones, shards, toys, trinkets, undecipherable scrolls. . . . Did the earth shake once upon a time, and swallow up my land? Did a tidal wave obliterate me and everybody else? If not, why do I await these cataclysms in sweating terror now?

There is a period when I lie wakeful night after night, staring at the tidal wave. It has already swelled over the edge of Britain, it is travelling, rising. . . . My father is in London, my mother, who is dining out, will be engulfed. I run to the head of the stairs and listen: all is silence, darkness, menace. I creep down to the library where one green-shaded oil lamp burns, which means that she has not returned. Duke the Great Dane sits in the bow window, frowning, listening: he seems as agonized as I. I clasp him round the neck and damp it with my tears; his sad cold yellow eyes look beyond me with complete indifference. Still, he permits me to lean on his brindled shoulder. Hours? minutes? tick away; till suddenly a great sigh heaves his ribs, his ears go up, he quivers: long before me he has heard the car approaching, and gives me time to hurry back to the night nursery.

The moon is my inconstant saviour; when she is in the sky she will carry me to dawn and safety. I mount guard at the bedroom window, wrapped in my eiderdown, intently studying her in all her phases. When, at the full, she queens it, I gaze hour long at her illustrious face. I cannot see the man in the moon. For me she is maternal, a story-book archetype like Mother Goose; yet at the same time she looks stricken, even aghast. Her rounded crooked open mouth is sending forth a call – one note, sustained, full-throated, that I strain to catch but never do. The whole world hears her in its sleep and never hears her.

She wanes inexorably, she is nowhere; and then I am alone with terror. The last trump will crash out and pull the black sky down and we shall all be buried. I sink to my knees and pray: 'O God, let daylight return and I will be good for ever and ever and love thee as I ought.' I creep under the bedclothes, within which more often than not sleep overtakes me and day is there when I wake up, and the thanks I render are perfunctory or nil. But I can remember winter nights when, tense at my post, I await reprieve with waning hope. My yearning for light is so intense that, when the first hint of it tinges the utter dark I think I am deluded. Not till a uniform dull pewter shade prevails, dividing the garden's masses from its airy spaces, do I hurl myself back into bed and sleep, as into a bottomless well. Remarks are passed about my pasty face and heavy eyes; but my explanation, namely that I have been awake all night, causes derisive laughter. Dickie says I used to colour up quite pretty, but it looks now as if I was going to grow up sallow like my grandmother. Each of these statements has its own appeal. *Cela vient de l'estomac* is Mademoiselle's verdict on all our ills and woes and quarrels; and a strong dose of calomel her remedy.

One day things come to a head in the matter of my stomach. I stand before the mirror while she attacks my hair with brush and comb and remarks, as usual, while she pulls and tugs: 'Il faut souffrir pour être belle.' Then, without any warning, a dagger pierces my abdomen. I give a loud cry, see my own reflection suddenly turn chalk white, collapse on the carpet, and go crawling doubled up along the passage towards the nursery, gasping and moaning, still with the comb in my hair and Mademoiselle holding on, scared out of her wits and urging me to rise. Julia takes over, becomes authoritative, gentle, puts me to bed and calls the doctor; Mademoiselle vanishes, escorting Helen to London to meet our parents for a pantomime – a treat I miss, but I feel, though out of pain, too ill to care. I hear Julia say: 'Don't upset their mummy,' and think bitterly: 'Not she. She'll just say I had a pain, she won't say I fell down dead; and if I say it I'll never be believed.'

What can have been the matter with me? I remember no sequel: nothing like that very early time when I sat on my mother's knee in a lovely white armchair covered with pink roses in the spare room; and was comforted for missing breakfast and told that Uncle Ethel* was coming in a moment to tell me to go to sleep: when I woke up he would have taken away my sore throat. 'Is he a doctor then? I never knew that!' God of gods among the uncles of my infancy, he comes in laughing: Apollo with his laurel bough; too bright for earth . . . (soon to be burned away). Never so happy in my life: my mother's arm round me, and him picking me up and giving me a kiss and putting me into the big bed. . . . I wake up again, not happy; in a hot muddle and being sick in a basin. But the funny thing is that a moment before I was in another room, one I have never seen before, and lying not in a big bed but on a narrow white couch; *white people* were round me, talking in thin murmurous rapid voices, quite unlike any I have ever heard. When I ask who they were, I am told I was dreaming. Where are my tonsils? Uncle Ethel has thrown

* The late Dr. Etherington Smith.

them away. Out of the window? Could they jump back into my throat? For a long time I fear so, and avoid the rose garden.

Nothing like that on the occasion of that inexplicable sword-thrust in my vitals; but – although the actual time-sequence may well have got telescoped and jumbled – it seems to have closed a cycle. Night watches, tidal wave, last trump, bilious attacks, calomel fade out. The moon remains, my semi-constant mistress.

7

The boathouse is another power centre, even more potent than the stables. Victorian-riverside-gothic, stucco and brick without, vaulted and pine-beamed within, packed with swallows' nests beneath the eaves, it is an oarsman's paradise. Racing craft, two tiers of them, inhabit it: the single sculler, the pair oar, the four, the eight; poised on rafters and stretchers like gold-brown giant hibernating insects. There is also the catamaran, and in winter the canoe, and a dear little light skiff which my mother can handle, and in which my father teaches us all in turn to swing our bodies, keep our elbows in, turn our wrists and feather our oars. The big punt, which is a kind of second home, remains through all seasons tied against the raft. Oliver the boatman presides over this realm. Stocky, cheerful, with a bristling ginger moustache and a geranium-pink face topped always by a dark blue cap, he gives out a powerful smell of shavings, varnish and sweat, and makes model punts and real paddles for us in his spare time.

The changing-room that adjoins the boathouse is bisected by a white canvas curtain on rings, behind which an enormous tin appliance for a shower bath affixed to the ceiling can discharge an ice-cold deluge at the pulling of a formidable chain. There is also a long lead-lined sink, and several taps and a number of papier mâché wash-bowls; also a W.C. with an unforgettable aroma – dank, earthy, mushroomy. On the near side, the changing-room has built-in benches along both walls, and pegs for rowing shorts and vests and towels. (For two years running a robin builds in the seat of one of the pairs of shorts, and we go in on tiptoe, peep and tiptoe out again.) Here we hurl our clothes off and dash into our bathing suits. Eased into the water by my father and upheld round the chest on a halter attached to a boathook I learn quite quickly, but not as quickly as Helen. Soon she can dive delightfully, proving to me that we do come up again if we go in head first; but I cannot risk it.

Often at week-ends or on Bank Holidays our aquatic efforts are acclaimed by trippers thronging the decks of Salter's River Steamers. Up towards Marlow, Reading, Oxford, down towards Cookham and Maidenhead glide these romantic and majestic vessels, packed with common people. They are dancing sometimes in a free and easy way, or bawling in chorus to the thump of a spirited invisible piano; or sometimes to the wiry, nerve-plucking tink-a-tink of a banjo. They drink beer and exchange

paper hats and throw crusts and empty bottles over-
board, aiming at the swans – a nasty vulgar habit.

Up and down, too, goes Colonel Poole, casting a boiled
eye upon us, doffing his straw boater to our parents;
spare, wizened, spruce, wielding his punt pole with
military precision; white-flannelled automaton, fanatical,
punting alone day long, spring, summer, autumn long;
mostly alone but now and then teaching a young lady
how to punt. The two ends of his moustache curve
downward to meet his chin like miniature ram's horns.
Colonel Poole is eighty ... then he is ninety ... or perhaps
a hundred ... I do not remember if he died.

It is boat-race time. My father is coaching the Cambridge crew. Wearing pale blue rosettes, we watch from
an appointed distance while gods to the number of eight
descend, how leisurely, upon the raft, their heaven-blue
mufflers wound around their noble necks; lower their
shining torsos, legs and arms, with what deliberation, into
their sliding seats. Then the unwinding of the mufflers,
the handing of them to Oliver and Godden, privileged pair
crouching to attend upon their going forth. Gently,
gently Oliver and Godden push them out; they paddle
off; the launch which has been quietly drifting in midstream bearing my father and his megaphone, and
several other figures of renown, is throttled back and
follows after.

Gang warfare breaks out all over Bourne End; partisan
frenzy leads to coarse tauntings, black eyes, bloody
noses. Rude boys and girls parade upon the towing path,

plucking off each other's pale or dark blue rosettes, stridently chanting:

> *Kymebridge the winner!*
> *Oxford the sinnerr!*
> *Put 'em in a match box*
> *And float 'em down the riverr! ! ! !*

or – horrors! – vice versa.

Cambridge will win, no doubt of that, my father is their Tender Shepherd. . . . All the same the amount of passion we expend is primitive and wearing.

On Thames's ever-rolling stream, against chill westering light and nipping winds the eight returns, the Sons of Time step out, lordly and casual, upon the raft. Their oar-bearing shoulders, their tumbled locks are of such melting splendour that I see them but dimly, through a fevered blur, before we are sharply withdrawn by Mademoiselle. Her response to them differs from ours but is as strong. Once as we walk glumly, sedately beside her past Townsend's Boathouse on our homeward way, one of the crew, in shorts and vest, bursts through the kissing-gate just as we approach it. A giant, ten foot high, almost touching us. We fall away before him and naturally he takes no notice of us; but as he starts to run on, Mademoiselle remarks in a clear voice: 'Mon Dieu, comme il est beau!' *And he turns*, he throws her a glance and a funny out-of-breath little laugh! He must have heard her! ! He must understand French! ! ! When, all of a twitter, we suggest this, she does not look embarrassed, but amused inside herself. Her face has gone pink and arch, quite unfamiliar. *Could she have meant him to hear?* She is wearing her new hand-knitted cream bolero with gilt buttons, her best skirt of violet serge, and on her head an enormous white cloth tam o'shanter with a jaunty quill above one ear. Her bosom and hips spring out above and below her waist with an hour-glass effect which we think repulsive: our lips curl when we catch her smirking at her figure in the glass. Surely he couldn't – could he? – like the look of her?

This is Mademoiselle's lucky day, and we do not grudge it to her, since the remainder of it will be our lucky day as well. No *devoirs*, no *punitions*. She retires to her bedroom, from whence issue sounds of humming and trilling. We sit by the schoolroom fire in our child-size rocking chairs and recite the names of all the loved ones and their sacred order in the boat. Which of them do we love best of all? Our inclinations vary; but one day by mischance we both settle finally for Stroke. Neither of us will yield him. Which of us shall have him? What about a double wedding? Yes! We will both marry him, we will have a double wedding.

8

Olive-silk-skinned river, pierced with reeds, weeds, water-lilies . . . long spiky reeds we tug and tug at till with a leap they come away from their mud anchorage: almost, they jump into the boat, half dry, half slippery.

We break them into sections and make darts by stripping down a piece of outside skin and shooting them over our thumbs. . . . Sick-smelling yellow lilies we are forbidden to pull up. . . . Sheaves of gold-brown ribbon weed that wrap insidiously round our swimming legs, that Godden cuts each year by means of a sickle tied to a boathook. . . . Large floppy leaves of lambent green that we call salad, that grow in the shallows by the raft, that we fish for, letting our arms wander slowly downward through the twitch of swarming minnows. . . . Swan-bearing river, nicked by the knife-edge of swallows' wings in their ever falling and soaring criss-cross patterns; grazed by the dark, solitary bobbers, vanishers – coot, moorhen, dab-chick – who swivel and splash in the distance and seem secretive and preoccupied.

Not so the swans, who are bold, greedy, unreliable. They thrust towards the raft and hiss and crane their snake-necks and noisily snuffle up the crusts we throw them, liking to see the bulges as the lumps go down. I wish they would go away: one blow from a swan's wing could break a man's leg, so why not all my bones? I can only appreciate them when they rock in midstream like abstract forms of peace and meditation, their cruel heads laid back against their sculptured pinions. Even so their blandness is deceptive. At any moment one or another of them will unfold; will ruffle and swell and gather itself and become a charging missile, a death ship propelled by fury up and down the flood. Strange that sexual urges so daemonic should end in such tranquil scenes of domesticity. When they go by in the late summer, each parent couple convoying its mushroom-coloured cygnet fleet, they look as complacent and respectable as a *bourgeois* family on a Sunday outing.

Regatta season: Marlow Regatta, Cookham; Bourne End Regatta in which Godden competes in the single sculling and loses by many lengths: we weep to see him cast himself supine, gasping at the winning post. But in the dramatic punt race, in which the competitors stand up in double rows and frenziedly wield paddles, his team shoots the post by a fraction of a length, and we cheer hysterically. . . .

Regatta nightfall, bringing the procession of illuminated boats. We sit snugly watching from the punt, along with two or three of the dear maids. Our decorations are frugal: a Chinese lantern in the bows, another in the stern; a single string of fairy lights is looped from limb to limb of the ancient willow (home of a white owl). We are aware that this lack of ostentation is deliberate, though it seems to us puzzling and regrettable. Downstream towards Cookham, we know, most of the river-frontages will be festooned with brilliant multi-coloured necklaces, blooming with rose and blue and lemon paper lanterns. Why should our lawn and celebrated boathouse not outshine them all?

Now come the boats; slowly, slowly, passing in procession; craft of the humbler creation, guided and propelled by half-glimpsed local figures of the riverside fraternity; small launches, mysteriously peopled, whose names we strive to recognize; and one or two so glittering that we wonder: can *actresses* be going by? For there *are* actresses, so we believe, secreted up and down the river banks, ambushed in thrilling house-boats. During the week, these dwellings seem deserted; but at week-ends, behind wee frilled muslin curtains and hanging baskets full of moss and pink geraniums, there are strong suggestions of romantic occupation. A high-pitched giggle . . . or a yawn . . . gramophones cawing and crowing . . . they are there, no doubt of it, although we never actually see a single specimen. There are gentlemen too, we know by the cigar smoke; and, once or twice, by a deep voice echoing from inner sanctuaries. Perhaps they never get up; or only come out after nightfall.

Last comes a giantess of a white steam launch, ablaze from end to end, crowded with opulent beings from another world: décolletée ladies, sequined, feathery, flowery; tuxedos; voices louder, less inhibited than ours. RICH AMERICANS!!!! For an American millionaire has recently built a vast black and white Tudor-baronial fantasy half-way between us and Cookham Bridge, and overnight laid out lawns and flower-beds, orgiastic beddings-out of calceolarias, lobelias, begonias and geraniums. He drinks champagne with every meal and bathes in it as well, they say. (My enterprising mother calls, we are proud to know, and later is bidden, and accepts to dine. Both parents say they had a most refreshing evening.)

But the supreme moment is still to come. . . . AH!

NOW! . . . THE GONDOLA! – at last. . . . Out she glides
from Abney boathouse, next door to ours, turns in
midstream, taking the current in one slow silent lingering
curve. Beauty, dark beauty, with sea-serpent-headed
prow, crimson-cushioned, burning on the water with
brilliant gold-and-blackness, symbol of tragic pride in
exile; not taking to our cheerful Thames with its lapful
of domesticated stars and dreams, its homely boats that
cast no shadow. In the glow of a Venetian lantern,
Giulio the gondolier is aureoled where he stands splendid
in white sailor blouse and trousers, with magenta sash,
and wide-brimmed black felt hat, just tilted. He leans to
his great oar in that inimitably noble pose, shoulders and
torso breasting the air again, again, one foot tapping out
the soundless hieratic rhythm. Giulio is a man to be
adored: tall, with mustachios, and a deeply graven, dark
yellow, melancholy face (he is homesick, has left wife and
little ones in Italy and cannot return to them till Autumn)
that breaks instantly into sparkling child-like pleasure
when my father hails him in his mother tongue. Their
voices, both musical, seem to exchange a singing dialogue
across the water.

Who are they in the gondola? As the great, carved
light-strung boat wheels slowly, we see them for a
moment: among them our parents who have dined at
Abney and are in evening dress. Do they see us? Wave!
No. . . . It is doubtful. They are surrounded, and look
different, going away, forgetful of us, with this nocturnal
gala, under the net of the enchantress. For strangely,

considering how close, as the years went on and right to the end of her long life became our friendship, based on shared confidences, sorrows, jokes, exhaustive scrutinies bent on the characters and motives of many friends and relatives, in those days I believed Violet Hammersley to be a witch; I feared she might change me or bewitch my mother. My tastes too tuppence-coloured to admire that elegance of hers in the high Spanish style which made her one of nature's works of art and caused all painters to wish to set down a reflection of her, I thought her very ugly. Her low-toned intensity in conversation troubled me; so did that hooded sombre gaze which impaled her interlocutor, especially when politics and finance were in question, and seemed to me literally to put out tentacles. When she played the piano, the energy and vehemence of her attack made me feel quite faint. Her troubles, actual, threatened or imagined, were more frequent, taxing and dramatic than those of other people. This was the period of elaborate after-dinner-party charades and she the star performer. Listening in my nightdress on the landing, the very echoes of them made my scalp crawl. But once I was privileged to watch her rendering of *Ta-ra-ra-Boom-de-ay*, to hear her daemonic stamp and shout as she circled the drawing-room with maenad locks unloosed and hairpins flying: Monstre sacré, Monstre de race, if ever there was one. . . .

Tonight she has flung a black lace mantilla over her raven's wing hair; the rest of her is white satin gleaming against crimson cushions.

Truly, looking back, I see that there were none of Beauty's daughters with a magic like hers; nor one in whom so much wit, wisdom, lovingness, forgivingness, strove with such autocratic failings, foibles.

The procession is over. A sky-invading medley of sounds reaches us from the fair: hoots, whistles, raucous, trumpeting dirges – the saddest of merry-making noises.

We shiver, yawn, do not protest when we are told that it is time for bed.

9

Ecstasy, anguish – the violent unpredictability and violence of Janus-headed life: this is the pattern graven on me; smiles, kindness, safe anchorage, turning within an instant to threatened trouble or actual catastrophe.

Our rabbits, Bunbutter and Tubface, in their cabbage-smelling hutches, leading monotonous but well-fed lives; other rabbits, skinned and slaughtered, enemies that must be done away with. Bluetits in the coconut, robins and all the other birds we feed in frosty winters; other birds hanging head downwards in the larder, waiting to be eaten. . . . River that threads my life with magic spells and symbols; river that, one day while I fish for minnows, shows me a something squatting in the water not six feet beyond the raft, arms akimbo, head a livid giant puff-ball. Calling Godden from the mowing machine I ask what it can be. 'Run away, Missie,' he says after a brief scrutiny. But as I reach the boathouse gate I hear

him shout to a fisherman anchored midstream in his
punt: 'My God! It's a man!'

Black-eyed Dora in the tobacconist-cum-sweet-shop
bestows her smiles on one and all. She is a beauty, and
everybody's favourite. She is so welcoming, and my
craving for sweets so compulsive that my visits are
constant, and make her laugh. Sometimes she slips me an
extra something with my penny bar, and then her full
lips widen secretly, like an amused Madonna of the
chocolates. One day I run, with sixpence, intending to
place half of my treasure in a tin and bury it in a pit I
have digged in the shrubbery, against a rainy day; but
the shop is shut. Why? It isn't Wednesday. And the
next day. And the next. Since my visits are illicit, it is
awkward to inquire. When the shop reopens, there is no
Dora but someone quite different behind the counter.
Next time I accompany my father to buy his evening
paper I remark to him that Dora seems to have gone
away. He agrees in a voice that gives me a foreboding
pang. Subsequently comes yet another of the times when
a school friend draws me aside and asks me if I can keep
a secret. The secret is that Dora is dead; she has been
murdered. She went out one evening with her True Love,
and in the field where the old brick-kilns stand he cut
her throat.

Her True Love . . . ? ? ?

10

Never imagine that children who don't say, or ask, don't know. In their blank eyes and heedless ears is hidden their attempt to make away with what they cannot swallow. Unable to become shock-proof except by cutting off response, they must go deaf and blind. Some remain so, learning self-protection all too well.

Myself in extremis, floored; myself saved, rejoicing: each of these opposed conditions deemed while it lasts, to be perpetual; yet even then a shadowy third, an onlooker, watching, recording, in the wings. . . . Perhaps this is an abstract of anybody's childhood. But of course it is only one aspect of the truth, or of illusion. On another level I went on quietly prospering in a temperate Edwardian climate; and since I was (apart from sums) very good at lessons, and good at running, jumping, climbing, also one of four tall, healthy, unusually good-looking children of devoted parents, I must have started with immense advantages.

The library is the unfailing heart of my security, and its portraits depict my indoor magic-makers. High up, commanding the room from an opulent gilt frame, hangs Robert Browning, bearded presiding Deity, painted by Great-uncle Rudolf Lehmann. By the look of his morning coat and the grey kid gloves he carries in a plump white hand, he is expected at some important public function. He has a cheery, purposeful expression, as of one prepared to march breast forward; yet he seems hampered by his formal togs. At the other end of this adored Victorian-Gothic room, appropriately facing Browning *père*, hangs a perfectly enormous canvas painted by his son, bought by my grandfather out of kindness so I understand, to encourage 'poor Pen' and soothe his anxious parent. Why is Pen poor, when he can paint such lovely pictures? This one represents a dear old French Abbé with a whimsical smile, clad in soutane and skull-cap. A tabby cat drowses upon his knees, and he is sitting at his breakfast table, enjoying a big steaming cup of coffee.

There are several other, minor deities, including Wilkie Collins in an overcoat with a rich brown fur collar. He looks spectral, with a bald dome fringed by grey fluff, and mournful moonstone-coloured eyes behind round spectacles.

On special occasions, such as Christmas or Hallowe'en or a winter birthday, comes the magic lantern. A white sheet has been hung over the french windows, and we sit in darkness, with thumping hearts, inhaling fumes of magic paraffin, listening to clicks and muttered curses from behind us, where my father struggles with the apparatus. All is well. A glorious multi-coloured pattern glows on the screen; then another and another.

Next comes a set of bright-coloured birds; then the tiger story, which my father tells while he slips in the plates my mother hands him – often upside down. Apart from a dim recollection of a happy ending with the

shooters routed and a string of tiger cubs emerging
from arsenic-green jungle I have forgotten this drama.
Then Bluebeard and his wife and Sister Anne, which
caused me such transports of terror and enjoyment that
no clear recollection of the slides returns. Last, Mr. Long
and Mr. Short appear; the one very tall and thin, the
other very short and fat; they whack each other over
the head with truncheons. And that is the end of the
performance.

At other times, on winter nights, we part the tapestry
curtains and peer out with a wild surmise; but there is
nothing in the garden, only the blank dark.

'Daddy, will the fairies come tonight?'

'No – no. I don't think so. Not tonight.'

'Oh, why not? Why won't they? Mightn't they? It's
not windy, it's quite dancing weather. Couldn't you
whistle for them?'

Presently he lays down his newspaper, extinguishes
his cigarette, and says: 'Well, we'll see. Just keep a
sharp look-out. And mind, not a sound. They're very
shy.'

He has to go upstairs alone, we know, to whistle for
them; our stomachs turn over with the suspense and
silence. We have almost begun to give up hope when –
ah! down they all come like birds in a white flutter.
Faintly illuminated by my father's lit dressing-room above
us, they dance on the lawn, they swirl and caper in a
jerky, spirited, rollicking, rather than a graceful fashion.
Then, as suddenly, they all spring upwards and vanish.

One night, one fairy is left behind. When my father returns we draw his attention to the white shape sprawling motionless on the lawn. She must be dead.

'No, no,' he says, somehow sounding tickled. 'Fairies don't die. She's just a bit winded by all that prancing. You'll see – she'll be gone in the morning.' And she is.

One day, during one of his absences in his constituency, Helen asks me sternly if I can keep a secret. While exploring in his dressing-room she has seen something behind the wardrobe. What? A long pole with lots of long strings attached to it, and on the end of each string a cut-out white paper doll. I do not twig, and she has to explain: the fairies! We are stunned. But chiefly I remember our pact to conceal from him and everybody else our prying and our shock.

We must somehow manage never to mention the subject again. No doubt he thought, with relief, that we had outgrown the fairies; and in the instant of our enlightenment, we had.

11

But Robert Browning remains numinous and so does the library, in the heart of which I imagine him and my father to be perpetually, voicelessly, in communication, mediating poetry to one another, the one from his armchair, the other from his lofty frame; weaving me also into the sacred web. Robert Browning is a great poet, and I consider my father a great poet, and I am going to be a great poetess.

For now I am eight, and certain of my destiny. I have emerged from mists and swamps and live voluptuous days, rhyming with inexhaustible facility. Suddenly one afternoon while I sit in the fork of the walnut tree, equipped with a bag of caramels and an empty exercise book, my blunt pencil starts writing as if by its own volition. At the same moment warm electric currents begin to stir and twist inside me. I look at what is written; and presently slip the exercise book into my bloomers through the elastic in the waist, swing down from the tree and hurry to find my father. I can't explain, and simply place the book open in his hands. He says mildly:

'Very nice.'

'Is it a piece of poetry?'

'Well, yes, you could certainly call it a piece of poetry. What makes you ask?'

'I made it up,' I say, choked.

He reads it aloud; and with astonishment I hear a stanza that strikes me as absolutely stunning.

> *Out in the shady woodland glade*
> *Where the wind blows soft and sweet,*
> *Where the leaves tell stories of wind and shade,*
> *And the acorn drops at my feet,*
> *I sigh as I wander amid the trees*
> *And my sigh comes back on the wings of the breeze.*

He does not say it is a banal bit of doggerel; he says it is a good beginning, and that I seem to have a natural feeling for rhythm, and that I must go on.

Go on? I need no pressing, I go on and on. No sooner a pencil in my hand than the tap turns and out flows another innocuous tinkle. Strange that this pouring out of words, this manipulating of rhymes and rhythms should so powerfully affect me – at times with fever and nausea – considering the superficiality (in retrospect) of the results. I composed nothing comparable in economy to a couplet of my brother's at the age of six, and already recorded in *Invitation to the Waltz*:

> *Too many things have we got to.*
> *Too many things have we not to.*

And nothing from the same deep level as some lines spoken spontaneously by my son Hugo, around the age of four and a half. We were walking together across a field on a day of wind and brilliant sun and chasing clouds. There came a sudden lowering of light and looking at the sky he said with dismay: 'The sun's gone'; then after a moment:

> *The sun's gone.*
> *The world is turning dull.*
> *We're falling through trees and houses and everything we walk on.*
> *The rocks won't balance.* (said with a pause between each heavy word, and stamping his foot.)

Shortly afterwards he said, without warning:

> *The clouds pass and pass*
> *Willy's lying in the grass.*

After which the muse deserted him.

I wrote nothing of this quality, but my father had faith in my talent and went on teaching me the rudiments of prosody and encouraging me to absorb good poetry into my system by memorizing large amounts of it: no trouble at all in those days. Once only did he hurt my feelings during that period of peak fertility; and even then the pang had more in it of surprise than of humiliation. My first narrative poem, entitled *The Lost Princess* opened on a sultry afternoon, the Queen asleep, the courtiers dozing, the parched birds clamouring for rain. My father read on attentively until he came to a line which ran: *'Oh for some lemonade!' sighed the King* – when he broke into a paroxysm of laughter.

Why?

Another, different sort of qualm came a year or so later with the composition, one night in bed, of a frivolous poem to amuse my sisters. It was a mere bagatelle in my own estimation – the account of a recent family journey to the Isle of Wight. But when I wrote down the verses and showed them to my father – himself a writer of superb light verse – he was delighted. He made me do a fair copy and took it to London and read it aloud at one of the weekly *Punch* dinners which, as a member of the permanent staff, he regularly attended. I was gratified to hear that his colleagues had made favourable comments; yet . . . I was uneasy. This was trivial stuff. Why not have presented one of my serious works – *Poppy Fields*, for instance, or *Fairy Gold*? Could it be that, although he praised these compositions, he had secret reservations?

And why, in times of crisis, or illness, do verbal jokes of his still pop up from nowhere and go echoing through my head? – verses dashed down in his handwriting in the Visitors' Book beneath the signatures of various 'Uncles'. One that begins:

> *George Duncan's wounds again are rawed,*
> *And if you ask me how, Sirs,*
> *You'll find the cause in Goldie (Claude)*
> *Who took – and wore – his trousers.*

A very brilliant mock-dramatic poem, of many stanzas. Another that runs:

> *Do you know Mr. Spedding (or Spobs)*
> *He is fond of his bedding (or bobs)*
> *His quality's such and we like him so much*
> *That we'll dance at his wedding (or wobs.)*

Affectionate tribute, this, to a non-uncle yet a frequent visitor, not altogether accepted in our hierarchy: **Mr.** Spedding whom his friends call Spobs, elderly dark-skinned bachelor, shambling, huge, who speaks in a soft falsetto voice from between thick lips and looks, we think, like an ogre, although he is always gentle, and fingers a rosary at certain hours, and must be driven to Mass (called Marsse) and reads holy books and would seem to be a holy person; also a sad and poor and lonely one.

Fragments of other verses return from time to time – things made up specially for us, or about us: not exactly funny but funny in a way, and with an undertone, like ballads, that is almost elegiac: for instance this hauntingly sad poem that we adore.

Two little dogs went out one day
When it was windy weather,
And to keep themselves from blowing away
They tied their tails together.

And the wind came down, and the rain came down,
And it blew, and it blew, and it blew;
It blew like razors and carving knives –
And it cut their tails in two.

And away, and away, like kites in the air
Flew those two little doggies about!
And one little dog was blown outside in,
And the other blown inside out.

And who can it possibly have been, *Up in the sky, Ever so high,* who

> *is pouring a canful of very cold water*
> *On the Green Man who married his beautiful daughter.*
> *But the green Man has opened his yeller umbreller,*
> *And says: I don't mind you, don't mind you, old feller.'*

What forgotten Chinese jar or plate or screen sparked off the Green Man story? All is lost, apart from this one vivid and mysterious fragment.

Where are the three little girls whose laughing portraits, sketched with such tenderness and such technical
grace of light long lines and short, and printed in *Punch*,
made us appear so cherished, comical and attractive?
Polly. Molly. Betsy. What has happened to them?

Quick said the bird find them, find them . . .

. . . They are only prints and echoes, all that is re-
capturable, among the other echoes inhabiting the
garden; lost paradise within which one master echo still
reverberates, as vibrant now as then.

Once upon a time, but when, in actual time, I have no
idea, a sudden searching convulsion of my whole ground
of being overtakes me in the garden. I am mooching
alone along the gravel path that runs between the lawn
and Lovers' Walk. It is autumn, and the sun has dropped.
I am not Amaranth Aurora or Beryl Diamond, or that
obsessive spell-maker, murmuring as I stroll or crawl
around OM MANI PADME HUM. I am almost no one,
kicking up amber drifts of chestnut leaves, aware of the
dark green thickets of laurel on my left, and on my right
of the hoary expanse of lawn, ringed by blue deodars
and cedars and already crisping with frost and sparkling in the opalescent haze of dusk. I look up and
see the moon quite high in the sky, a moon nearly at the
full, singular in its lucence. I stop to stare at it. Then
something extraordinary happens. . . . A flash . . . as if
an invisible finger had pressed a master switch and
floodlit my whole field of vision. At the same time the
world starts spinning, and I am caught up in the spin,

lifted, whirled. A voice splits the sky, splits my head. . . .
And yet there is absolutely not a sound in the garden,
not a barking dog, not a shunting train, not even a late
robin; and although the detonation is within me it is
also immeasurably distant, as far beyond the moon as I
in the spinning garden am immeasurably below it. It is
the Voice of God, of this I am certain. He has addressed
me, he has pierced me with a word, an arrow with my
name on it, imperative. . . .

All over in a second. I am put down again; dropped
out. I hurry back into the house, hoping not to be seen
because I must look different. I dash upstairs and seek the
mirror in my bedroom; scrutinize my poorly lit reflection.
. . . Not changed.

God has pointed at me. He has not touched me.

PART TWO

She turned away from me, and she went through the Fair;
And fondly I watched her move here and move there;
And then she went homeward, with one star awake,
As the Swan in the evening moves over the lake.

Tradititional

1

What I have put down so far might almost be called sub-autobiographical. It has been like a descent into a vault or cave or crypt, where all is darkness when you first penetrate. Then a torch flares, light is thrown here on a painted fresco, there on a carving or a bas-relief: figures in a landscape, real and recognized, yet each with the mystifying impact of a symbol-in-itself, pure of interpretation and interpreter; and able to be caught only just on the outward side of verbal or pictorial existence. Any attempt to treat the findings, or to expose them to more air and light might cause them to vanish altogether.

In between this subterranean record and what is still to come lies, I suppose, all the material for an autobiography proper; but it will never be written. For one thing, I have never, for long, kept a diary, and my memory for facts and dates is unreliable. Also, the considerable amounts of letters and papers I have hoarded seem too intimate for print – at present. For another thing, so much of my 'life story' has gone, in various intricate disguises, and transmuted almost beyond my own recognition, into my novels, that it would be difficult if not impossible to disentangle 'true' from 'not true'; declare: 'This is pure invention. This

partly happened, this very nearly happened, this did
happen' – even if I could conceive it to be a worth-while
operation.

I am, of course, not unaware of the essences, the
fertilizing images and names and faces behind these
novels; though why some fused and proliferated, and
some did not, is another matter.

The clamour of 'spotters' – friends, non-friends, critics,
acquaintances and perfect strangers – on the scent or in
the know is doubtless an occupational trial for writers of
fiction. We bring it on ourselves; and it is foolish and
naïve to be unprepared for it as well as hypocritical to
swear our total innocence. But in my case, I suppose
because much of what I wrote dealt with romantic and
sexual love seen from a subjective angle, the detective
squads were rampant; also the self-identifiers; also those
with a so-called knowledge of my private life more
beady-eyed than accurate.

Dusty Answer, my first novel, uncorked a torrent of
letters, literally hundreds of letters – chiefly from
America in the beginning, later chiefly from France –
explaining that I had written their own unhappy love
story: how could I possibly have known or guessed it?
More than one lesbian lady urged me to abandon my so
obviously frustrated heterosexual life and share her
hearth and home. One young Frenchman withdrew to a
mountain-top and there typed out a two hundred thou-
sand word sequel to *Dusty Answer*, accompanied by
photographs and letters designed to prepare me for our

joint future, when he would teach me love. And so it went on, with twists and variations which it might be tedious to multiply. It was one of those curious, unaccountable explosions of the *zeitgeist*.

A triangular situation in another of my novels had certain parallels with a situation of which I was ignorant at the time of writing but which in fact later affected me closely. I was accused of exposing, exploiting it, causing embarrassment and bleeding hearts. Did I invent the fictional 'plot'? – or subconsciously sneak up on what was going on unknown to me, and reveal the gist of it under the guise of fiction?

A character called Mrs. Jardine that I once created, generated from a fusion of youthful impressions of relatives on the paternal side, has had five different 'real life' models attached to her, all ludicrously wide of the mark, three of them unknown to me even by repute.

Etcetera, etcetera, etcetera.

Perhaps it would not have been too conceited to tell myself that at least these characters, and others, must have been 'alive'. But an incurable ambivalence developed in me with regard to my profession after the smash-hit of *Dusty Answer*. It seems comical in retrospect that this impassioned but idealistic piece of work should have shocked a great many readers: but it did. It was discussed, and even reviewed, in certain quarters as the outpourings of a sex-maniac. Of those who had known me as an innocent child some were utterly dismayed. How could I have so upset my mother? And indeed my

mother, ever loyal but ever prone to believe one or other
of her brood about to overstep the mark with fatal con-
sequences, was startled and torn in her feelings. Was it a
blessing, or one more matter for wild and vain regret
that my father had long ago embarked upon his last
tragic illness, and could not follow his daughter's disconcerting fortunes? Girls should be pretty, modest,
cultivated, home-loving, spirited but also docile; they
should chastely await the coming of the right man, and
then return his love and marry him and live as faithful,
happy wives and mothers, ever after. All this I knew and
was by temperament and upbringing fervently disposed
towards; assuming (or half-assuming), with Mrs. Gaskell,
that 'a woman's principal work in life is hardly left to
her own choice; nor can she drop the domestic charges
devolving on her as an individual, for the exercise of the
most splendid talents that were ever bestowed'. But I
seemed already to be losing grip on the dual responsibilities of my destiny. Unhappily married, childless,
separated, wishing for a divorce; and now all at once,
good heavens, one of the new post-war young women
writers, product of higher education (Girton College), a
frank outspeaker upon unpleasant subjects, a stripper of
the veils of reticence; a subject for pained head-shaking;
at the same time the recipient of lyrical praise, of rap-
turous congratulation, of intense envy, of violent con-
demnation, in the contemporary world of letters: a world
I had burst into unawares. In those days I knew no other
female writers, young or old; with the exception of May

Sinclair whose novels excited me, I was singularly ill-read in fiction published in the twentieth century. With the Victorians I was well acquainted. I thought of the nine-teenth-century literary giants as my great ancestresses, revered, loved, and somehow intimately known. So I remembered how acutely they had suffered from censorious and sententious critics, and when hot flushes, faintness, nausea, loud rapid heartbeats afflicted me, it was a drop of comfort to feel, if in no other sense their match, at least sisterly in suffering with such noble souls. Also, I thought with yearning of the androgynous disguises, the masculine masks they had adopted for the sake of moral delicacy; of the unimpeded freedom to immerse in the creative and destructive element which anonymity had bestowed on them... might have bestowed on me? – on me, in whom rectitude, stern puritanic principles inculcated by my mother strove ever with an ardent, pleasure-enjoying, love-hungry nature; on me, who always got in my own way, and of whom there seemed, now that I was an author, far more, a far more unmanageable amount than ever. Where, oh where was my place in the lofty scheme of things entire? What with the general post-war fissuring and crack-up of all social and moral structures, coupled with the abject collapse of my private world, it was easy to fear I was nowhere.

Perhaps it was all this, and not true humility, that caused me to respond to praise and generous encouragement with a sort of anxious shrinking, a suspiciousness that soured the taste of simple satisfaction and gave to gratitude and budding confidence a tenuous, half-quenched glow. 'Don't read me, don't speak of me,' was partly what I wanted to reply. *That is not what I meant at all. That is not it, at all.*'

2

Having written down these lines half unreflectingly, I was struck all at once by the way in which the poetry of T. S. Eliot went on dropping into my head without premeditation. So I took down and re-read the *Four Quartets*, that sublime, unhopeful, consoling cluster of poems; and discovered, or rather rediscovered, that everything was there – everything that I have been trying, and shall be trying, to say: about the intolerable wrestle with words and meanings; about the way *words crack and sometimes break, under the burden . . . slip, slide, perish . . . the knowledge that every attempt is a wholly new start, and a different kind of failure;* also that *There is only a limited value In the knowledge derived from experience; The knowledge imposes a pattern and falsifies.* . . . He has mapped out this area of the human predicament with words impossible to imagine losing resonance or decaying with imprecision. It would be absurd, presumptuous, to attempt to emulate his words; and equally presumptuous to go on ransacking his soul's explorations to fit my purpose. All the same, there must be affinities; or so I venture to think.

Certainly I have not – or I hope I have not – lingered

so long around that first house and garden solely out of
self-indulgence; and I have tried to eliminate all the
words and forms that seem to lack resonance, or the
essential gesture. Certainly that moment in the garden
under the silence of the moon and the blaze of the
announcement does remain eternally present; although
years, years upon obliterating years will pass before, on
a loop of time's spiral I pick it up again and find myself
still there, hidden excitedly . . . and still astounded.

Go, go, go, said the bird: human kind
Cannot bear very much reality.

Certainly one day, but that is far in the unimaginable
future, I shall be forced to bear the ultimate in unsup-
portable reality; and also, strange but true, the voice of
a bird will draw me through the moment of transition
into the moment of release from action and suffering:
into being; into a reality I, somehow, must have earned,
although it was too bright to bear for long – or I too dark
to bear it.

3

Only once afterwards did a visitation at all comparable
descend upon my childhood; but this second time it
was on quite another, less 'interior' level; and the surprise was that misery could be arrested, consolation
instantaneously received plumb in mid-welter of torren-
tial woe.

We are in the Isle of Wight for our summer holiday: in the Bay of delights I have described before, in a story called *The Red-Haired Miss Daintreys*, and must not linger over now. It is September; late afternoon, stillness and hot sun, the prawning rocks exposed with their limpets and gold-brown streaming fleeces; also the low-tide belt of sand, firm, damp, with ripple-patterns carved in it, and over it a film of nacreous liquescent blue. Bare-legged, my holland frock tucked into my bloomers, I paddle, voluptuously, with stealth, in the warm rock pools, insert my prawning net in likely cavities beneath the swaying slippery seaweed fringes; wait; draw it forth, scrutinize my haul: jumping or scurrying marine minutiae, bright-coloured tiny shells and pebbles, a strand of coral or rose or viridian mermaid's hair: everything is precious.

I am hailed from beyond the Life Boat Station and start to wander back with pail and net, to where a curiously formal-looking family group is waiting on the front: my mother in a dark coat and skirt, a hat with a veil . . . Helen also with a hat on, wreathed with clover, and a tussore 'dust coat' . . . my father, not smiling. . . . Long before I reach them my choking sobs and moans burst out, precede me audibly: I realize what has been kept from me till now I suppose, or so under-emphasized that I am taken unawares: namely that this is the day and now the hour when my mother leaves for America, to see Grandma, taking Helen with her; they are about to embark on the Ferry for Southampton, leaving me,

Beatrix and John in my father's care, with Julia at the helm. I have been prawning away in cheerful ignorance while they plot and carry out betrayal, lock trunks, put on smart hats and prepare to abandon me . . . for ever. I wish to cast myself upon my mother, dare not approach her, see her face alter, note distress and anger on my father's face, disgust on Helen's, start to run off madly. . . . In a loud, emotion-fraught voice my mother calls: '*Now Rosie!*' . . . appealing and threatening. What a shock! I stop at once; stop crying, absolutely at once. She has vanished, with Helen (how? did Mr. Reason's fly remove them?) They are wiped out, both of them. And I am indifferent, full of serene indifference, looking forward to high tea with shrimps. 'Come along,' says my father, still looking rather pale and not best pleased with me. I mount the steps in the cliff face behind him; and at the top, on the Turf Walk, decide that the moment is ripe to turn his attention to my whisking pail. But he is looking at the sky, now crimsoning with sunset.

'What an extraordinary cloud,' he says.

Indeed, an extraordinary and marvellous shape of vapour hangs above the bay, a vast archangelic silhouette, snow-white, softly suffused with fire all through its outer edges; with a suggestion of bright hair streaming backwards from a bowed, rapt head, and long down-pointing wings.

'Extraordinary,' he murmured. 'Miraculous.'

He is smiling faintly now, but his voice is talking to himself, not me, and I say nothing, wondering if he feels sad and why I do not. Already the angel is beginning to lose radiance. A gash like a toothless grin appears in the region of the head, part of the wing shreds off, dissolves. . . . Now it looks more like a sky-riding witch, with a hump and a cloak.

Our kind of family would not go into seaside lodgings nowadays (they would perhaps be motoring across Europe with Moses baskets and collapsible cots and gear and togs innumerable), but in those halcyon days before the break-up of the western world it was not unadventurous to embark for the Isle of Wight and for a reckless month invade *St. Winifred's* or *Dinwiddie* or *Boscobel* with their horsehair sofas and chairs, and enthralling photos and texts and oleographs, and their unforgotten smells of cooking and dried pampas grass and seaweed, and their interestingly stuffed mattresses that amused my father (an excellent sleeper) not my mother, and the kippers, the mutton, the apple dumplings. . . . He seemed to enjoy the eccentricities of lodging house *moeurs* as much as we did, and was a particular favourite with landladies.

That evening, after visiting Boy in his small bed, he presided while we demolished eggs and bacon, bread and butter, shrimps and jam; and with a view I suppose to giving a cheerful keynote for this interlude, remarked:

'Rosie's the head of the family now.'

'Then I'm the hair of it,' said Beatrix, my five-year-old sibling, in a flash.

Julia, whose mood was definitely euphoric (no interference for a month), clapped a hand across her mouth. My father exploded in a long burst of laughter I can still remember.

I didn't think it all that funny.

4

There is a saying that the island 'draws': people who once visit it keep on coming back. We did, certainly. The native inhabitants still have a built-in island flavour, a special warmth, cheerfulness and courtesy not apparent in the mainland. They are not always strictly beautiful; but I have noticed how often the children of Light disguise themselves behind crumpled or crooked faces and shrewd little eyes that wear strong spectacles, and dry, warm humorous voices such as theirs. Perhaps the regal auras of Charles I and Queen Victoria still lend the island air a higher vibratory frequency; perhaps the murmuring shade of Alfred Lord Tennyson still brushes the birds, and the tides; perhaps the vestiges of pre-history scattered over and beneath its turf and chalk and sandstone account for the magical atmosphere of certain woods, downs, valleys, chines, undercliffs and standing stones. . . .

I was pleased to discover, fairly recently, that Totland was not so named, as I had feared, because of its amenities for tots and toddlers. It is very ancient, and means a sacred or holy piece of ground. Once, a year or so ago, I was sitting where I am sitting now, watching a pair of woodpeckers in the garden and hoping for a glimpse of the red squirrels, when I felt suddenly *caught*, as if in a magnetic current. Such a strong sensation of *being watched* assailed me that my skin crept. All my imagination, very likely; but I jumped up and almost ran through the french windows on to the lawn.

Whoever it was came with me, hurried me hither and thither, as if I was expected to be searching. But what could I be looking for? Now my small garden seemed full of noiseless laughter, mischievous, non-human . . . swirling with it. Next moment I stooped and picked up from a corner of the rose bed a roughly heart-shaped stone object: a flint: an unusually pretty and delicately finished Stone Age implement with a pronounced cutting edge along its smoothly polished matrix. The back, which was uppermost when I first saw it, making it look like a tiny pale-shelled tortoise, was scored all over its surface with a faint but definite criss-cross pattern, and pierced round the perimeter by tiny holes, like pin holes.

When I showed it, shortly afterwards, to a guest, I could only insist: 'It wasn't there before. It couldn't have been. I couldn't have missed it.' My guest did not contradict me, or mock me.

That is the unembroidered story of my flint. It is beside me now. I am no psychometrist, but I like to hold it.

5

The Isle is also supposed to eject those whom it does
not fancy. Be that as it may, it went on harbouring us,
year after year, and indeed generation after generation.
My mother brought my father, in a bath chair, to be
benefited (was he?) by the mild sea air, for as long as
journeys were possible at all. Helen and I both came as
young married women, with our children. Later we
came back, each one of us, in a more solitary and occasional way, chiefly to visit Mrs. Hammersley. It was at
her suggestion that after my mother's death I bought a
piece of land above her enchantingly pretty *bijou*
property and built on it, to the design of David Stokes,
her son-in-law, the little house to which I sometimes come
alone now, *pour le recueillement*; and sometimes with my
grandchildren.

Originally I intended it as a sort of wedding present
for my daughter Sally: somewhere, if she and Patrick
went on living abroad, as seemed likely, they could
return to; a refuge always waiting for their children.
She was pleased at the prospect; but she never saw it.
Strangely enough, I was there, measuring for carpets and
curtains, when the news came from Java. I will not dwell
much on the period between their departure in 1957 for
Jakarta and her death there on midsummer eve in 1958.
For one thing their brief married life has been told by
Patrick in *The Perfect Stranger* and there is nothing I

77

should, or want to, add to his account. After she left
England my life began to sag, to sicken, as if a slow
internal haemorrhage were sapping it. Sometimes as the
months went on a grey fog seemed to be coming towards
me from the future; it made me gasp for breath. I
supposed I was missing her acutely and putting a good
face on it – or trying to. Nobody seemed to notice anything much amiss with me: though once or twice it came to
my ears that I had become 'difficult', and this frightened
me unaccountably: as if people might know that I had a
dreadful disease which I myself only half suspected.
Sally's letters were long, regular and vivid, full of her new
activities, delighted with new scenes, new friends; stoical
or humorous about domestic difficulties. Why did they
give me such a pang? Why was I, in my innermost sub-
conscious, always expecting to be summoned, always
half preparing in secret for a flight to Java? Why, each
time I saw the word Jakarta did I feel as if I'd been
hit hard in the solar plexus? Perhaps these feelings are
usual and natural in mothers whose children have gone
abroad, especially if they go to places where the political
situation is disturbed and the climate notoriously un-
healthy. Still, they were not natural.

However on this June evening, 1958, the grey fog had
disappeared. A friend was with me and as we crossed the
Solent and I pointed out to him the long low fawn-
coloured bulk of Hurst Castle on its curious sandbank, a
memory of Sally at four years old flashed on my inward
eye. One long ago day in April I had hired a fishing boat

and set forth with her and Hugo for an expedition to Hurst Castle. We never got there: the weather became squally, the Solent choppy ·and presently worse than choppy, the motor began to splutter and ccnk out. Half-way towards our destination I requested our skipper to turn without delay and make for the shore. He became taciturn and, I suspected, nervous; obliged to take to the oars he rowed in silence doggedly, with an occasional glance at the inky storm-cloud overtaking us. I sat with Sally on my lap, making a show of enjoyment to prevent her from becoming frightened. Then to my horror we shipped a wave or two: I wrapped her in another oilskin and tucked her under the tarpaulin in the bows. Hugo, preserving a nautical on-the-job detachment, was baling steadily, and I baled too. Each time I glanced at her, I saw a plastered fringe, a sopping, radiant face, as round, rose-pink and lambent as a huge wet rose, peeping from beneath its tarry hood and laughing at me. Not the shadow of a doubt or quaver on it . . . utter delight and utter trust. . . . None too soon, we were safe in the shelter of a bay, and I extracted her, still beaming; and then we were thankfully stepping out on shore. Casting an appraising eye on sky and sea, Hugo remarked that the weather had been against us. On her he cast the glance I was to see often in their early days, directed towards her or towards Piper our Cairn terrier: patient with, but weary of, frivolity.

This scene came back to me those many years later, as we crossed the Solent. I wondered, supposing we really had been going to drown, could I have taken her through it without fear? I thought yes, perhaps I could have . . . and then a vivid spirit-image of a child would have remained there; a laughing ghost, like Supervielle's Enfant de la Haute Mer. . . . These thoughts, of course, were idle, superficial.

We visited Mrs. Hammersley and took her for a long drive along the coast and then inland. She enjoyed motoring in the way a dog does, with total disregard for drivers' fatigues and hazards; relentlessly, insatiably. An exceptionally light-hearted evening followed: I decided to leave all measurements and other building matters until next morning, before the drive back to London.

Since Sally was nearly always in my thoughts it is no wonder that, as I prepared for bed in my hotel room, looking out over the sea towards the lights of the mainland opposite, another memory of her should have slipped, very quietly and clearly, into the forefront of my mind. Once, when she was five years old, as we walked together on the downs above Compton in Berkshire where we spent the war years she said, without the slightest warning:

'One day . . . one day . . .'

'What about one day?'

'One day I might call you and call you and call you . . . over the whole world. Over the whole world, and you might not answer. What shall I do then?' Her voice seemed to toll. Taken aback, I quickly promised her that I would always answer.

'You mean you won't die?'

'I mean I won't die.'

'Promise?'

'I promise.'

'That's all right then.'

She dropped my hand and ran far ahead of me, humming a tune. We were hunting for the pasque flower. Often and often as the years went on I returned to that scene, that hour. Who was it in a child's body suddenly adopting such a voice? How could I have promised her that I would never die?

She never mentioned death to me again. She was not a questioner by nature; not hot for certainties. Most of us are born lost, and searching, – I for one. But she was born found. And out of some unique inner well of her being she would occasionally speak in ways and words that it was impossible to forget. She was four years old when, watching me pack up her cradle to send it to a friend, she murmured 'Stop' as I was about to lift the cradle proper off its base; touched it carefully, set it swinging, said with a rueful smile: 'I wish I could get in and have one more rock before I have to grow up.'

The cry of the human race . . .

When she was six, perhaps seven, the war and the break-up of our home obliged me to send her as a boarder to her little school on the hill, with its far view over downs and beechwoods: idyllic-English-pastoral. She was to be happy there and greatly loved; but the night before the morning of her first term away, when I stole in to see if she was asleep, a voice, the same 'changed' voice, came out of the darkness saying: 'Beautiful maiden! How can I bear to be departed from you?'

Yes, I was thinking, but not sadly, of all these things that night in 1958: something in their quality seemed to sum up the ground of her mysteriously simple nature. No, it was not unusual to have her thus in my mind's eye and ear: one's children, and indeed one's grandchildren, constantly stir about in one's imagination like an accompaniment to daily living. There was no premonition of disaster in the memories. On the contrary, I was happier than usual; not troubled, as I sometimes was, by my last sight of her, as the train drew away at Waterloo, looking intently at me from the window, not waving, white-faced.

Next morning the weather broke. It looked like setting in for heavy rain, but it was still no more than threatening when we drove to my nearly completed little house. It looked 'all wrong' that morning, not promising at all, with builders' planks and rubble half-blocking the approach, and no flowers growing in the muddy garden. But when we went in I was agreeably surprised, and in my mind's eye started to plan the furnishing and decoration. I was kneeling to measure the space between fireplace and kitchen door when there came a loud, sudden thud on one of the french windows.

'What was that?'

But my companion had wandered off and I was alone in the empty room.

When I got up a few moments later, I looked out and saw on the paved terrace beyond the tall glass door a dark blot upon the stone – a dead bird, a young black-bird.

I cried out: 'Oh!' and my companion returned, and looked, and said: 'Oh dear! Sad. Broken neck. How did it happen, I wonder?'

'It's only just happened. I heard a great thud and — It must have flown straight against the glass. But why?'

'Didn't see it I suppose, poor thing. There's every excuse for not spotting a great piece of very clear glass – particularly a young bird trying its wings.'

'How horrid. Do you mean it'll always be happening? I wish I hadn't. . . .'

I couldn't bear to look, and couldn't look away. This account is strictly factual; and the plain truth is that on the instant of my seeing that lifeless shape a thud fell, leaden, upon my heart. It seemed such an unpropitious omen; so very strange. . . . What was it I had heard or read about birds as messengers? I felt depressed now; but I went on measuring and discussing; and then it was time to go.

We went out by the glass door, and I had to look again. With the same sense of being transfixed I said: 'I can't leave him like that. Will you put him under there?' I pointed to a thick tall shrub of laurestinus at the farther end of the pavement.

I said it lightly, and to humour me my companion picked up the small body and placed it gently on a bed of dead leaves under the shrubby branches. I added lightly: 'You know what it's supposed to mean: a death in the family.'

Saying it aloud seemed to remove the sting. All the same, why hadn't I been able to pick it up myself? I had never minded touching dead birds.

When we got back to the hotel, the manageress told me brightly that my son had telephoned from London and left a message asking me to ring back as soon as possible.

A few minutes passed; and then his voice on the other end of the line said that Sally was dead.

PART THREE

'Who then devised the torment? Love.
Love is the unfamiliar Name
Behind the hands that wove
The intolerable shirt of flame
Which human power cannot remove.'

Little Gidding, Four Quartets
T. S. Eliot

1

Nowadays I measure my life by Sally, not by dates.
There was the time before her birth; the time of her life
span; the time I am in now, after she slipped away from us.
The decision to write about it has not been easily arrived
at; but I am not the first person, and shall not be the last,
to undertake a similar testament; and, like others, I
can only go forward in the hope that the great glimpse
(what can I call it?) which overwhelmed me at the peak,
or nadir, of my agony may taste as unquestionably to
others, as it does to me, of reality; and therefore will
interest those who have had parallel experiences; may
even just possibly (thought I do not really expect this)
rouse a faint query in one or two minds closed fast in the
'intellectual' dogmas of negation. But my overriding
motive is the longing to bring comfort to those in
affliction as measureless as mine was when joy so suddenly surprised me.

I published the nucleus of this mystical experience in
Light, 'the oldest psychic Journal' in 1962. But this
seemed to myself like speaking in a whisper to the con-
verted; half guilty and apprehensive, half sheepishly
thankful, that I was bearing witness through a channel
unlikely to catch the eye of my customary 'public'; or

of such of my friends and relations who suspected my goings-on and were too tactful and respectful, too embarrassed, too repelled, or simply too indifferent to question me directly on the subject. In 1962, although in a sense 'recovering', I was still foolish enough to be vulnerable to the atmosphere of social dismay, discomfort, pity which bereaved persons are apt to engender.

Common sense is apt to desert such persons; and I was only just beginning to realize what AE, the Irish mystic, poet and seer, discovered many years ago and told his friend – and my friend – Constance Sitwell: namely that 'he had found it better not to talk of these things often, because either people thought one mad, or it frightened them'.* I was unable either to remain appropriately dumb or speak out steadily about my new knowledge and my investigations; and consequently I was racked by a sense of doubly betraying the loved and vanished child; and was doubtless felt to be very awkward socially when, lacerated almost beyond bearing, I strove and stammered to explain why the idea of distraction, or of change of scene – those vain panaceas recommended to all mourners – was odious to me.

If speaking caused such consternation, how could I ever expose myself, or her, or the forbidden subjects, Death and Survival of Death, nakedly in print? Yet the forbidden subject, with her as the beating heart of it, engrossed me altogether, day and night. All other themes

---

* *Conversations with Six Friends* by Constance Sitwell.

in all the books pouring from all the pens and publishers around me, all newspapers and broadcasts and intellectual quarterlies and weeklies seemed to me now – to me who had once read them with absorption – full of sound and dullness, signifying nothing. I was still moving about in worlds not realized, and the loneliness of this, the sense of exile, caused a well-nigh total seize-up in such powers of self-expression as I have. Only those born with, and then traumatically deprived of the generative current, the instinct to create in words (or of course in any other medium), can know the strangulating spiritual blockage which such a dislocation can produce. Perhaps purer, more dedicated, less feminine artists, stronger characters, cannot be thus deserted. Perhaps the cause really lay in what I have written earlier about my relationship to my own work. Perhaps, too, it is something gained to be able to enter into the anguish of those compelled to suffer without the capacity to heave up grief in words, mould it and put a frame round it. All I am sure of is that inquiries for my 'next book', however solicitously meant and gratefully acknowledged, could only act as one more turn of the screw. At times I had the actual physical sensation of a solid book-like object bound in stiff boards with cutting edges and sharp corners stuck in my midriff. Sweat, groan as I might, I was stuck with it for ever.

To purchase and fill an assortment of notebooks with surreptitious scribblings – memoranda, notes, recollected images and sayings, copies of scripts obtained, of letters

from her to me, from me to her, mysterious almost daily
happenings that seemed to defy any but 'supernatural'
explanations, records of dreams . . . and visions . . . was
some alleviation. They made up an underground hoard
I fed on, brooded over, starved on furtively; and although
there seemed no possibility of fusion and proliferation
in the fragments, nothing that reminded me even faintly
of my one-time identity, my former capacity to energize
them, at least, when pressed, I could say: 'I *am* writing',
without feeling much more than usually disheartened by
the equivocation.

And even at the very worst, I was upheld by an inner
voice quietly telling me to wait, trust, keep still, submit
with patience to every aspect of my maimed existence.
I was not really being idle. The step in knowledge I had
taken, though elementary, was so vast that even if
sterility proved permanent and I was labelled once and
for all a manquée figure – why should I mind? What did it
matter?

Also, now and then I would become aware of silent
laughter, hers, indulgently mocking me, not at all sorry
for me, loving but mysteriously amused, as if she were
saying: 'I laugh where I am. *Laugh too*. Remember the
patience of the universe.'

2

I have never been, and have not become, what is called
a religious person; at least, not in any orthodox theo-

logical or churchgoing sense. At the time of Sally's
death, while remaining theoretically open-minded I had
finally cut myself off from any form of spiritual search.
In my teens I had had the usual spiritual twinges which, in
my twenties, and after marrying an atheist, and subsequently another one, I had attempted to discard as in-
fantilism unworthy of a forward-looking adult in this day
and age. I was careful not to voice those dim stirrings in
the company of those to whom I looked up, intellectually
speaking, as my pastors and masters. These were, almost
to a man, to a woman, if not bigoted atheists, confirmed
rationalists, humanists, materialists, agnostics. I wished
to emulate those whom I most admired in a life dedicated
to the arts, to aesthetic appreciation, to the cultivation
of personal relationships. Noble ideals, indeed. . . . Alas! –
I knew only too well that I could never achieve their
stoicism in the face of death: death which to them spelt –
and still spells – unquestionable extinction. To me, death
was the dread, the intolerable, implacable arch-enemy;
and how to come to terms with him, except by believing,
with Donne (*Death, Thou shalt die!*) and Browning (in
Prospice for instance) that he could be truly overcome
was beyond my powers. Nothing I had heard from
pulpits, nothing I had been told by orthodox Christians
of any denomination sparked a response in me. The
Anglican Burial Service was of heart-rending beauty; so
were the words of the great mystics of the east and middle
east and west, when they wrote of death and immortality . . . but were they true as well as beautiful? . . .

All doctrines, dogmas, ceremonies and rituals clerically dispensed seemed to me meaningless. If all these invocations, these abject placatory addresses from miserable sinners to the God of Wrath, these vestments and other concrete symbols veiled the immaterial essences of Divine Revelation, then I could never hope to grasp them. Faith was a gift, a capacity which the fortunate few were born endowed with – like perfect pitch, or a genius for mathematics: enviable, but not to be acquired. To my mind, one thing was incontrovertible: *if* God was, whatever God was, He did not listen to our supplications. The Creator was indifferent to His Creation. All the same, one had to choose the good; one had to cling blindly, not knowing how to justify it, to the validity of the concept of a moral order in the universe; to the paramount importance of love for one's fellow-beings: because loving was connectedness, and this was as essential to staying alive as bread and water. The state of not loving was the state of atrocious exile from the human situation. I hoped that this creed would prove enough to keep me on the rails and see me through (see me through what, to what? – I dared not face the question): I feared that it might prove insufficient. During bad times I knew it would: the void advanced its tentacles to suck me down. But better times returned: and when they did I told myself severely: 'Missed it again by the skin of your teeth. Don't push your luck. Take a cold look at yourself skidding, skimming ... or next time you'll be caught for good, and done for.' But there were always plenty of distractions.

In short, I was a privileged person and also a deprived one.

What did I mean by this 'It' that I was still managing to by-pass? . . . Something to do with some sort of great examination I was failing in and failing in. . . . Yet if anyone had said to me; 'Metaphysics is simply common sense, organized common sense. When you get men separating subjects, separating sciences, separating science from religion, religion from psychology, philosophy, etc., the vital link is lost. To insist on separating subjects is to insist on death for them because it involves ignoring what is, ultimately, their breath of life. Only from a metaphysical standpoint do things make a whole.' If anyone had addressed me thus my whole being would have cried out: 'Yes!' and followed. At least, I think so. . . . But I hadn't yet met anybody likely to address me thus.

There was just one intuition that I could not smother, contrary to enlightened rationalistic blueprints for the prospects before humanity. Just as we continue to be swayed in secret by superstitions from which we proclaim ourselves delivered, so I went on privately clinging to the fancy that 'I' would not, could not be extinguished by bodily death. That much of wistful hope, indeed, had lingered on in the climate which had nurtured me. My father had bowed, I imagine, but how unexultantly, to Darwinism; his elegiac poems continued to reflect his classically other-worldly, dreaming self. My mother, like George Eliot, 'strenuously rejected all prospect save in the mere terrene performance of duty to our human kin'.* Both belonged to that 'rearguard of steadier and sadder thought' of which Frederic Myers wrote; and wore their agnosticism (again like George Eliot) in the manner of a spiritual shield.

Hugo says he is not at all afraid of death, and I believe him – though heaven knows what, if anything, he expects 'on the other side'; but I think Sally was afraid of it, as I was; and it is the bitter and lasting self-reproach I have to live with that I failed to prepare her or to reassure her. How could I, being so blind? I found out afterwards that she was terrified at first, after she had left her body. The possibility of dying young had never crossed her (conscious) mind; and like countless human beings who 'go over' suddenly, more particularly in the flower of youth and vigour, she stubbornly refused to believe that she was 'dead'. It was her fierce struggle to get back that, within a few days of earth time, woke me up: she shouted for me, and in the darkness we shared I heard her; and then I was able (though with what bungling and confusion!) to go through her death with her, rather in the same turbulent, inept (on my part), stepped-up, breath-stopping way in which we went together through her birth. It was part I suppose of the lesson we both were compelled to learn. Which of us was it worse for? God knows. She understands things now which I still only half apprehend,

* Autobiographical Fragment. Collected Poems. F. W. H. Myers.

and she has forgiven me; but it is not easy to forgive myself.

3

When I came round from the anaesthetic that late afternoon in January, 1934, there was no nurse or doctor in the room. She and I were alone. I heard her before I saw her. She was making strong, broken noises of protest, sorrow, from some unidentifiable region near my bed. 'Yes, yes. I know,' I said. 'Never mind. I know. . . .' Immediately she was silent, listening. In this soundless naught, recognition started to vibrate, like a fine filament, between us; quickened, tautened. I swung in living darkness, emptiness; in the beginning of the deepest listening of my life.

When, probably quite soon, Sister came in and said loudly: 'Here's your baby, dear – a lovely daughter – don't you want to see her?' I started to sob: I suppose for happiness. There were shadows over her birth time and the period before; and I had not been able to imagine a joyful conclusion to these unreal months. Particularly I had schooled myself not to expect a daughter, which was what I longed for.

4

There were no notable events in Sally's short life, and she would be the first to ridicule the idea of a biography.

95

Patrick Kavanagh, her husband, has captured the essence of 'his' Sally in *The Perfect Stranger*, and without reference to this beautiful memorial, what I am attempting now is to conjure a fragment of my own vision of her.

Though extraordinarily simple she was by no means unsophisticated: such a phrase as 'manquée figure' would have been coldly rejected because it smacked of heartlessness; and because she never had any truck with dismissive, modish attitudes and judgements. I never have known and never shall know anyone more incapable of snobbery in any of its guises. I was inclined to think her too obstinate in her loyalties, especially to crooks, cripples, neurotics and lame dogs in general; but now I think that the truth was that she was simply much more charitable than most of us, far more capable than most of genuine compassion, so that labels fell off and categories dissolved when she was present, and quite nice people emerged from under them, disarmed by her humorous, not unastringent trust in them. She was angered by meanness, spite and petty malice; puzzled and chilled by the values and connivances of calculating gentry (she came across a few); shocked into sick, pale-cheeked, brooding dumbness by falseness in word and deed, double dealing and other varieties of emotional treachery.

She was obliged to witness a catastrophe of this nature at close quarters, and at an impressionable age. A pattern of relationships she wholly trusted in collapsed without warning; she saw the effects of this upon a person she had been accustomed to love happily. Unable to swallow what confronted her, she withdrew for a time into herself and suffered deeply; equally, for fear of contagion, I set a distance temporarily between us. This perhaps was the most hateful aspect of the full reckoning I was trying, and failing, to contend with. I don't think she ever lost her basic confidence in me; but it was then that her dependence on me vanished, never to return. Perhaps it would have happened anyway; no doubt it is better in the long run for all children that they should not believe in an unshadowed world of human love; but it is sad, and dangerous, when they have to be shocked out of it so violently and with such affronts to innocence. *Almost a mercy killing.* . . . A few years ago I came across this phrase. The poem in which it occurs is, if I remember rightly, a philosophical justification of ruthless destructiveness in certain relationships of love. I was particularly struck by the word 'almost'.

If I touch upon this period of her life with me it is because the thought of anything bland, any sentimental blur in Sally's outline is unthinkable. Her home life in infancy and early childhood; then after the break-up of my marriage with me and her brother; and later with her father and Cristina her stepmother, was on the whole a very happy one; but there was one season in her budding time when a killing blight might have – did almost – touch her. Her flowering when it came seemed all the more vivid and miraculously unflawed. For the rest, it was the idea of her, so sound, so whole, the intolerable thought of her growing up infected by the world of corruption, moral indifference, psychosis, breakdown, drugs, drink, suicide and so forth which enabled me to fight off – by the skin of my teeth – the temptation to despair. Her face, candid, wounded, pregnant with silences, went on shining faintly, a golden disk, at the far end of a dense claustrophobic tunnel.

Somewhere, somehow, not in this life, these complex and dreadful wrongs must be redeemed. Whoever needs forgiveness, Sally will need none.

But she was not a pliant character; and she would not easily have come to terms with the world's ways. Unable, perhaps, to compound, she might have become formidable in that old age of hers which I was never able to imagine. There was a granite streak in her. She was a richly feeling, not a romantic person. To romanticize her image would be to falsify it. The capacity she had for developing stubbornness, for instance, was a family joke: Miss Resista was one of my nicknames for her. Some readers may remember the pre-war, gravity-defying music-hall artiste of that name.

She had an excellent brain, a scholarship brain, and great powers of concentration. She might have got a first in her final (English) schools at Oxford; just failed to do so. This was the only time I saw her shed bitter tears of disappointment. No doubt the distractions and intoxications of being an Oxford beauty had triumphed too thoroughly over the academic curriculum; but when I re-read some of her essays on Wordsworth and on

Shakespeare, I am surprised by their maturity and insight. Clothes she adored, and parties, and going abroad on very little money, and the company of girl friends and being surrounded, as she was from seventeen onwards, with boy friends and suitors. She was absolutely incapable of double-crossing a friend of either sex: that is why, no doubt, there never seemed to be any jealousy poisoning the air for long around her.

One of her tutors told me that, in discussing Sally with another tutor, she had said:

'Sally is the goodest character I've ever come across.'

'Not *good*,' said the other; 'The most beautiful.'

She told me this some time before her death; not after it.

One night, strolling back late, and alone – illicitly I am sure – from someone's rooms to her own college after a party, and carrying a bottle of unopened sherry, she was accosted by a drunken American in air-force uniform. Unable to shake him off, she lifted the bottle, felled him with a well-aimed blow on the head and left him in the gutter. I was extremely disturbed to hear next day of this encounter; but she shrugged it off, unruffled.

Her greatest natural gift – her voice, a pure and potentially radiant soprano, seemed the one she set least store by. Perhaps if she and Patrick had not met at Oxford and decided to marry, she might have returned to Milan and resumed the training so auspiciously begun the year before she went to Oxford. But I think not. Despite the glowing prognostications of her teachers (particularly the male ones) she always rejected the pressure I tried to put upon her as absurd. She had the voice – and I the dedication! Perhaps it was lack of confidence in her own powers; perhaps a just self-assessment; perhaps, since – although never 'bohemian' or insubordinate – she was naturally inclined, like her father, to lean towards anti-Establishment, she may have seen the prospect of a serious musical career as a threat to her freedom to impose none but her own self-disciplines. Or perhaps she was aware, in some deep layer of her consciousness, that she had other destinations and not much time left.

She had a way of laughing that I never met in anybody else: completely silent, head thrown back, as if she was tapping some primeval source of laughter. This is a memory of the later years. She was a serene child, and became a clown to amuse the brother to whom she was devotedly attached: not a laughing child. Literal-minded, taking to heart (at the age of six) his accusation that she lacked a sense of humour, she purchased a book of jokes and riddles and bent herself to master its contents. The success of this venture surprised as much as it delighted her. Seeing him roll about, speechless, with low groans, as she read from her manual, she felt that she had got the hang of jokes.

All the details I treasure of her beauty – the ravishing lines of her lips in smiling (the archaic smile – she really had it – its mysteriously subtle curve), her rather gliding walk, her odd slow buoyant grace when she

danced, the something unforgettable about the model-
ling of her eyes and eyelids – their extended outer
corners, the grey-blue large iris flecked with green, the
cut of the luminous lids, like segments of magnolia petal
. . . such images seem to set her in the antique world; in
some golden age of plastic and poetic harmony, meaning,
beauty; startling me now only a little more profoundly
than they always did.

But at the same time she would wish me to say that
she was not very pretty as a little girl, and, if engaging,
rather fat and greedy; and that though in her eighteenth
year she began to fine down and achieved a lovely long-
legged slim-waisted figure, she always had round shoulders. Also that she was very short-sighted. Perhaps this
partly accounted for her dreaming expression; and for
the fact that, although wherever she went she drew all
eyes, she seemed unconscious of it. She thought (rightly)
that she looked plain in spectacles, and wouldn't
wear them, except for work, or driving a car, or in the
theatre.

In the last few years of her life, particularly after her
marriage, she did look like a young corn goddess. Sometimes, though, her nimbus faded; sometimes she looked
pale, with darkened eyes and bluish shadows in her skin,
like an emerging, not yet sun-lit Persephone.

Dedication Poem, the last poem Patrick was ever to
write for her in her life-time caught this archetypal
golden girl, and at the same time intimately personalized
her.

Curled in your nightdress on the beach,
Corn-yellow ghost, pale with sleep,
Head to the starry North, bare toes to the burning East,
Tracking the sun's climb into our sea-side perch,
I watch you at the fringe of this other island
Our public love makes private for us two;
Your face in floating shadow, like a moon,
Stretching your arms around the bay to yawn,
Ebony trees in your fingers turning green . . .

If I do not quote the whole of this poem it is not so much because he has already printed it in his own book, where it truly belongs, but because the last few lines belong to 'his' Sally. These that I have quoted show her *sub specie aeternitatis*. The poem 'wrote itself' he told me afterwards, a few days after their return to Jakarta from a holiday in Bali. On their last night, they had slept on the dazzling powdered-coral beach by the edge of the sea. He woke up early and wandered off to watch the sun rise; came back and watched her. . . . He was puzzled, disappointed, he said, because when he put the poem in her hand she did not smile. Unknown to either of them – and all unknown to me of course – she was already beginning to be preoccupied by the initial on-slaughts of the relentless invader, poliomyelitis: onslaughts which, five days later, were to stop her heart – her superbly strong heart which, almost up to the last hour, seemed likely against all odds to pull her through.

Despite that soul quality of hers which I have suggested, which, as she grew up, was to become her secret password to the ranks of young girls loved by poets, who die young, to be celebrated by their lovers (ah! how many, in how many anthologies, in how many languages and times!) – I never dreamed that harm could overtake her. Wherever she went in the world she was at home; her artless magic worked to make her cherished. Did she ever have an enemy? – I think not one. Still, why did I imagine she was immunized from danger? What *hubris*, I think now.

'If only there was a heaven, Sally was made for it'; 'the one real hope of our generation'; 'so much better than any of us', 'ineffable'; 'her angelic face'; 'she helped me so much – I don't know how to go on living now she's dead'; 'Sally was my idea of a saint: if only I believed in prayer I'd pray to her as well as for her'. . . . Such extracts, which could be multiplied by dozens – incredulous, horror-struck, passionately resentful, extravagant perhaps – from letters I received, prove something of the impact she made upon her contemporaries.

Two brief obituaries are hers: one in the Cranborne Chase School Magazine:

'There never was a member of this school more lovable, loving and gay-spirited than Sally. She enjoyed to the full all she did, especially music (she sang beautifully and played the violin) and her academic studies. She had a special gift for making friends and keeping them. Hers was a rich and rounded personality that shed warmth and light

103

on all who knew her; for this there is deep cause for joy and thanksgiving, as well as for mourning.'

The other, in *The Indonesian Observer*, 25th June, 1958, wrung my heart even more poignantly:

'Mrs. Kavanagh was not only endowed with the natural gifts of beauty and intelligence but was one of the few who used her talents for the benefit of the community. Many Indonesian ladies were studying English under her able tuition, and she also gave classes to Indonesian personnel of the Shell Company.'

How the success of those classes delighted and amused her. How polyglot they became and how they snowballed. On her last day of active life, in spite of a bad headache she went out and took a class, rather than disappoint her pupils.

As for her gifts to me, her mother, they are beyond reckoning. From her birth onwards she was La Consolatrice: to borrow the title bestowed upon another incomparable daughter, that Stuart princess, child of Mary Beatrice of Modena and James II, who died in 1712, at the same age as Sally.

She was a born letter writer, pouring herself out on paper from the age of eight onward in comments and descriptions penetrated with her particular warmth, solid intelligence, humour and sensibility. It is tempting to quote numbers of them; but I will only reproduce a portion of the last one I was ever to receive from her. After the usual inquiries – so unperfunctory always, so shrewd and sympathetic – for certain members of her

family, and after a list (not unusual!) of requests: 'a
couple of nice Italian shirts, some material for a cocktail
dress, plain because everyone wears florals', and one or
two other items, she goes on:

'Well – Bali – it was the most glorious and perfect
holiday and is the most *fascinating* island. I am at a loss
how to describe it because it must be unique in the
world. We stayed in a little village with a sort of local
Sultan who has turned his palace into a guest-house. The
palace consists of a series of courtyards filled with
flowering shrubs and joined by huge intricately carved
archways. Each courtyard has one or two little thatched
bungalows, quite self-contained, where you live and eat.
The Sultan himself is inclined to come bouncing along in
sarong and turban plus European handbag just when you
are settling down for a lovely read. But he was very in-
formative and knew exactly what was going on every-
where. The life is extremely primitive but also extremely
intricate. It is a real community life and the worst offence
you can commit is not to join in. Everybody is a farmer
and the whole village helps each member with his rice
fields. The numerous painters, sculptors, carvers are not
professionals – they do these things in their spare time.
If one of them gets a big commission and hasn't time to
farm his fields, the rest of the village all contribute some
rice for him and the money he earns usually goes to build
some new temple for the village. Then there is a tremendous amount of music. In the tiny village we were in, there
were two orchestras – one led by the Sultan's (or the

Tjokorde's) nephew who is a composer also. One day he thinks of a new theme and practises it all day with the chief xylophonist. When they have mastered it they bring in the next best xylophonist or a gong player until finally the whole orchestra has learnt it. The orchestras are composed of sleepy-eyed peasants just back from the fields, and they practise every evening. At any moment a filthy little girl may wander on to the floor in their midst and start to dance; then she will leave just as abruptly. She scampers on and she scampers off, but while she is dancing she seems disembodied – completely serious – completely dignified. I found the music and dancing tremendously exciting. We saw several performances with the dancers dressed in gold-embroidered costumes with vast floral headdresses. One night the Tjokorde had a performance in one of his courtyards. There was a full moon and the arch was dotted with flaming candles. It is an extraordinary mixture of formality and casualness. Nobody bothers to sweep away the leaves; children and dogs wander about among the dancers; the dancers themselves abruptly come and go; the orchestra sits cross-legged in a semicircle, chewing betel-nut; never any applause. But all is grace, dignity and beauty as well. One night we walked for hours across the paddy fields by moonlight to a tiny, very poor village where the dancers couldn't afford the full costume. We sat on a bench with staring children pressed against us and really felt ourselves to be in the heart of the country for the first time. And oh! what a beautiful walk, with the moon reflected in the rice fields! It involved going through a monkey forest, but rather to my relief the inhabitants seemed to be asleep.

'Another day we saw a harvest festival procession. Four different processions of girls dressed in orange bodices, green and purple sarongs, all bearing offerings on their heads. The offerings consisted of everything to be found in a rice field, piled high and beautifully arranged: dried frogs, eels, fish, and rice itself in so many different forms and shapes that you would never have thought it was rice. When the processions met, the dancers who had been weaving in and out of them performed their dance in the centre of the cross roads; and then the whole cavalcade went slowly up over a bamboo bridge into the temple. Here the offerings were placed in a huge mass with banks of flowers all round; and the floor of the temple was a sea of orange tops and brown faces, chanting prayers, laughing, staring at us, gossiping, while the priests threw the holy water liberally over them. Later came dancing to a fourteen-man flute orchestra – ghostly, haunting music.

'The people are extremely beautiful. But the most impressive thing is the strength of the religion – a Balinese form of Hinduism. *Everything* is religious, and religion is an integral part of everyday life. Every rice field has a shrine piled with offerings. Every festival (and there's one nearly every day) is basically religious. Whenever they make any money it goes towards a new temple; wherever you eat, somewhere in the corner you will come across a banana leaf with a few grains of rice in it for the gods.

'Our bungalow was opposite the tooth-filing pavilion; and the first thing pointed out to us on arrival was the pavilion where the corpses are laid out. The greatest ceremony of all is the cremation – an occasion for tremendous rejoicing. Usually people wait for a big-wig to die – someone bound to have an expensive cremation – and then they all dig up their dead and pile them on too!

'The last two days we moved to a lovely hotel by the sea where our bedrooms opened on to the tropical beach. ... You can imagine how sad we were to leave and come back to Djakarta.

'I nearly forgot to tell you! we flew over a volcano with a bright blue lake burning in its midst! ! !

'Masses and masses of love,
                    Sally.'

Apart from its intrinsic merits as a letter from a traveller, it shows – as all her letters always did – how wholeheartedly she enabled those she loved to enter into her life wherever she was absent. It arrived two days after my return to London to find Patrick's cable lying on the floor inside my flat; and when I saw the envelope my first thought was that it was all a grotesque appalling nightmare and now I was awake again. Then I did not dare to open it; but presently I had to; and then such extraordinary vibrations of life, vitality, exhilaration seemed to come out of the thin pages that, for a few minutes, I was caught up in them and almost happy.

I will not make a chronicle of the ensuing days and nights. There are no words there. There never will be.

5

A fortnight later, a friend whom I will call by his initial, J., drove me to Oxfordshire to spend the week-end with close friends of his and mine; I will call them L. and R. The evening of our arrival was spent in talking about Sally. All of them loved her dearly. I was unable to stop weeping; yet I began to feel, somewhere in my being, a tremor of relief and reassurance because they appeared to believe me, genuinely to believe me, when I went on insisting that I knew she was 'not dead'; that she was 'near me', 'as much alive as ever' – scarcely grasping what I meant myself. At first I had been afraid that they were being merely kind and soothing; but when L. said quietly: 'Of course', the tremor started. Later when we went up to bed, she described supra-normal experiences following a shattering bereavement in her own life. Had she always been certain that life continued after death? Yes, always. Nothing more certain. Hers was the first voice to make me feel that I was not alone, or out of my mind, perhaps.

But I did not, could not mention the phenomena which underlay my urgent insistence on Sally's livingness. I was scarcely even examining them consciously. They seemed perfectly natural; yet at the same time impossible. They were physically and yet not physically experienced; appearing to occur in a body with perceptions which were mine and not mine. For instance, on (I think), the third night as I lay half awake, I was . . . how to describe it? – lifted up: lifted on huge pinions out of my mortal dungeon; or perhaps a better description would be that a Great Breath blew me upwards, a giant bellows! . . . I had Sally by the hand and we took a great leap together. Another night, I thought that someone invisible brought her and laid her quietly beside me in bed. I didn't dream this. I didn't see her or speak to her; but an extended sense of touch informed me that she was lying beside me for some time. Another night, I became aware of my father, who died in 1928, standing by my bed with an air of wanting to address me urgently. He looked as I remembered him in his middle years; and the heart-wrung concern for me I sensed in him caused me to try, wordlessly, to reassure him; also to thank him for this desperate effort to come back on my account. I knew what it was costing him; I was as full of gratitude as grief; and not at all surprised; and when, presently, he was not there any more, I felt a pang like homesickness; but also relief, for his sake.

Yet he had not 'materialized', I did not physically see or hear as L. with her Highland blood had seen or heard. It was an interior happening. Needless to say, at that time I had never heard of the subtle or the etheric or the resurrection body; or of astral projection;

or of the scientific likelihood that countless forms, worlds within worlds of them, are invisible simply because they are travelling on different energy levels, or at different vibratory rates; and because our physical eyes are designed as instruments of limitation.

To return to the week-end: that night passed, and so did the next morning. In the afternoon, my friends went out for a walk, leaving me behind to rest. As all bereaved people know, grief is inexpressibly tiring; and I was thankful to fling myself down on my bed and be alone; thankful too that in spite of feeling prostrated with fatigue I was still in a frail state of mental calm. A blackbird was pouring forth his whole being just beyond my window; and from where I lay I could see elm tops moving against an intensely blue sky in billowing masses of unearthly greens and golds.

Suddenly, a clear high-pitched vibration, like the twang of a harp-string, crossed my ears. I thought: 'This again . . . what is it?' – remembering that I had heard it before, very soon after the news came: in fact, that it had preceded that sensation of being 'lifted by the Breath', But this time, instead of being transitory, the sound settled into a strong, rising and sinking hum like the sound of a spinning top. At the same time a sort of convulsion or alarum struck me in the heart centre, followed by a violent tugging sensation in this region. As if attached to an invisible kite string that was pulling me out, out, upwards, upwards, I began to be forcibly ejected from the centre of my body. I heard myself moan, felt a torrent of tears pour down my face, distinctly remarked to myself that this was like some very peculiar birth process; registered phenomenal occurrences deep inside my head: it seemed that my eardrums were being plucked – literally plucked and shaken – as if they were closed doors that must be shaken loose: my hearing was being freed, I suppose, and it was a difficult yet painless process. Then the humming faded out, and the song of the blackbird, swelled, swelled, as if it was being stepped up a hundredfold. Never could I have imagined notes of such wild, piercing purity and sweetness. For a while I did hear that bird – I must have heard him – with liberated ears.

I was drifting and floating now . . . but where, and for how long? There is no way of telling. Perhaps for only a few seconds of earth time. A passage of symphonic music, jubilant, penetrating, vigorous, crossed and receded from me like a wave. Was I picking up, supra-sensibly, from the ether, an actual performance going on somewhere at that moment? There was certainly no gramophone or radio switched on in the house: I was entirely alone in it, and it stood by itself, surrounded by barns and garden, the building nearest to it being the small ancient, village church. Whatever I heard seemed at once familiar and unknown. As I write, I can recall its melodic outline, but I cannot recognize it.

Now I was with Sally. She was behind my left shoulder, leaning on it. Together we were watching Patrick. His face, only his face, confronted us: it was clearly recogniz-

able but the whole scale of it was altered, expanded;
and it was self-luminous, and transformed by an expression of dreaming beatitude. He was (we both knew)
starting on a journey. I said: 'Aren't you going with
him?' 'No,' she said, 'he's got to go alone.' I said: 'I
expect he's going to D.' – (one of his closest friends, at
that time a novitiate in the Dominican Order.) Again
she said: 'No'; and added: 'He'll go to Auntie Peg.'
This is the name by which my sister Beatrix, the actress,
is known to all her nephews and nieces. I am anxious
not to make hard and fast interpretations. All I want to
say is that, in those early days, I held to the entirely
erroneous supposition that Patrick might decide to
retire from a world become intolerable. It never occurred
to me that he might choose to become an actor, as well
as a writer. Although he had been prominent and success-
ful in various amateur productions at Oxford he had
rejected the idea of the theatre as his profession. However, two years after his return from Java, he suddenly
decided to throw up his job in a publisher's office and
joined the Salisbury Repertory Theatre: thus, as one
might say, 'going to Auntie Peg!'

Patrick's lit face vanished, but Sally and I remained
together, wordlessly communicating. More than anything, it was like laughing together, as we always did
laugh; like sharing the humour of a situation: his going
off without her in some sort of state of disarray and un-
preparedness. . . . She made some characteristic joke (I
can't define it) about the muddle of his packing. I did not

see her. I had the unaccountable impression that she was hiding her face, that I was forbidden to look round. There was no light, no colour, no external scenic feature: only close embrace, profound and happy communion; also the strongest possible impression of her individuality.

Then, with no shock or sense of travelling, I was back in my body, awake, cheerful as if I had just replaced the receiver after one of our long gossiping joking conversations. I lay drowsily, trying to piece my 'dream' together . . . then in a flash remembered. Now for the bite of the steel-toothed trap. . . . Prepare, accept, understand . . . But it did not spring. Memory stayed in sweet tranquillity on the fringes of consciousness. If I was conscious of anything that I ought to scrutinize or question, it was my glimpse of Patrick. He looked so very splendid, so handsome and happy; why on earth had I thought him so shocked, so ground into the dust, that I had hardly dared to leave him in London and come away for two nights?

I looked at my watch and found that over an hour had passed. I sprang up, went to the window and looked out . . . and beheld a visionary world. Everything around, above, below me was shimmering and vibrating. The tree foliage, the strip of lawn, the flower-beds – all had become incandescent. I seemed to be looking through the surfaces of all things into the manifold iridescent rays which, I could now see, composed the substances of all things. Most dramatic phenomenon of all, the climbing roses round the window-frame had 'come alive' – the red, the white. The beauty of each one of them was fathomless, – a world of love. I leaned out, they leaned towards me, as if we were exchanging love. I saw, I *saw* their intensity of meaning, feeling.

I came downstairs to join the others. I couldn't think of anything to say except: 'I've had a wonderful rest.' L. glanced at me and said: 'You look as if you had.' Later she told me that she wondered if it was an hallucination that I suddenly looked about thirty years younger.

After tea, J. took me for a drive through the midsummer countryside. What a drive! The sun shone powerfully among full-sailed somnolent cloud-galleons; but the light suffusing earth and sky was not the sun's: it was a universal, softly gold effulgence. Hills, woods, groves, clouds, cornfields, streams and meadows – all were moving and inter-lacing buoyantly, majestically, as if in the ineffable rhythm and pattern of a cosmic dance. I was outside, watching the animating, moulding eternal principle at work, at play, in the natural world; and at the same time I seemed to be inside it, united with and freely partaking in its creativity.

Astounded; awestruck. . . . Awestruck, astounded. What words are possible? *And yet*, the sense of recognition, recollection, was predominant. Again and again I told myself: 'Yes. Yes. This is reality. I had *forgotten*.' There seemed to me nothing peculiar in having a double set of senses: I mean, that I went on observing and registering with my customary five wits, and now and

then making ordinary comments about – what? . . well,
what? – about the landscape and the weather, and
country houses, and our friends.

It struck me, at one moment – how thankfully! – that
whatever was happening to me, I was having visual experiences the very opposite of those I had had under
mescalin about eighteen months earlier. That world had
been hard-edged, semi-petrified, and yet with a reptilian
potentiality of movement. The spectrum had shrunk for
me, and I could discern only greyish-greens and vague
browns, and a curious *vin rosé* pink. A fine gloxinia in a
pot became an artefact, a wondrous object carved from
jade and snowy rose-tinged quartz; silk and woollen
materials assumed sculptured folds; faces – or, anyway,
the two I saw – turned into stone images, ancient, eroded,
with crafty satyr-like expressions; hands lying still on
lapidary trouser legs started to lengthen and crawl
slowly, like some crustacean form of life. One of the
pictures on the wall – a large still life in which a reddish
blur in the background suggested a coal fire in a grate,
became stereoscopic. The table was solid under its thick
crimson cloth, the fruit was made of onyx, the fire in the
grate was flickering and leaping out to scorch me with
tongues of flame. In short, out of mere curiosity, and
with the minimum of supervision I had entered a
magician's cave within whose claustrophobic precincts
disconnected material phenomena evoked in me cold
admiration or irresponsible hilarity; no love, no shared
enjoyment, not even much alarm, despite the crawling

hands and the acute pain in my sinuses and somewhere in my rib cage. *Then* I had been trapped in hallucinations and, alas! in loss of sensibility; *now*, accountably but certainly, I was seeing through the illusions and limitations of my physical senses into a world of light.

That evening, talk sparkled and rippled round the table as if the unimaginable death which had drawn us together were – not forgotten or ignored, but somehow overcome; so that we could tease each other and be teased as usual. No, not as usual. Our laughter seemed to bubble up from some primordial spring of well-being; like an echo of the laughter of the gods. I am not sure when it was in the course of the evening that I became consciously aware that the room was ablaze with light: a white column of incandescent light was vibrating between floor and ceiling – visible, I suppose, only to my opened eyes; but it never occurred to me either to remark upon it or to doubt that it was there, objectively present. Behind the dazzling screen it interposed, the faces of my friends occasionally seemed to dematerialize. I watched one of them, and was surprised, as well as touched and amused, to see that the countenance, instead of being on the square and solid side, had become almost transparent, and seraphic-looking, set on a long graceful neck.

All things were pleasure to me and nothing could grieve me. . . . Truly for twenty-four hours I knew the mystical meaning of those words: still know it, inasmuch as that

117

glimpse remains, and always will remain, enough to live by, in sure and certain hope that the end is joy.

But by contrast, the light, or rather no light of common day when it returned was insupportable; and the worst was still to come.

I suppose I had imagined that after plumbing the depths of suffering I was saved: that I had been set rocking, endlessly rocking, in an aerial cradle between two worlds. I had to learn, and re-learn, and learn again day after day, week after week, month after month, that I was truly left behind to crawl on as best I could, eternal exile, through the stone streets full of other people's daughters. Only indoors, in solitude, could I draw breath. That summer, a van with a loud speaker attached to it began to tour the Square in which I live; a voice shattered the air repeatedly, calling on people over twenty-one to come somewhere or other for their POLIO JABS. This commodity had just become available to Sally's age-group. . . . On the other hand, sometimes – and increasingly as the months of the first year went on – when I opened the door of my flat, a cloud of incomparable fragrance would greet me. What was it ? – what could it be ? At first I wondered if the old lady then living on the floor above me had begun to use some exquisitely perfumed bath essence whose echoes were somehow penetrating my rooms through the ventilating system. But the old lady went away, and still these exhalations pervaded all the air with an unearthly aromatic sweetness – spicy, yet delicate and fresh; compounded of lilies?

clove carnations? frangipani? – and something indefin-
able as well. .... It was not for me alone, this fragrance:
I mean that it would, I think, have been quite perceptible
to others; only, but for Patrick, I was so often alone in
those days. However, I remember that Laurie Lee came
in one evening, and after standing for a time in silence
said three words only: 'Now I believe.' He had been one
of the most passionately resentful of all those who loved
and mourned her. I should add that he was acknowledging
that the mystifying and pervasive scent I had mentioned
to him was there, indubitably: I know nothing about his
beliefs in the wider sense. As for myself, I don't know by
whose agency this sign was given to me; much less how it
was brought about. I only know that it was so; and
therefore once I was sure of it, I murmured my thanks
each time I came back into my empty flat. Months and
months afterwards Sally referred to the phenomenon
through two separate and independent psychic channels;
but although these 'channels' have now become among
my dearest friends, to whom I owe a debt of gratitude
impossible to repay, I will not emphasize them further
here. They will understand why this is not a 'psychic'
book, but simply a personal record. Sally would be the
first to laugh if I were to write that my alleged daughter
together with certain other alleged discarnate entities
named and unnamed appeared to be producing, or
attempting to produce, certain types of materialization
not unfamiliar in the annals of psychical research; but
that since the evidence offered was merely hearsay and

therefore unsatisfactory, the possibility of fraud or self-deception could not be excluded and the whole case was clearly useless from the point of view of the s.p.r. As I say, Sally would laugh; and I have great respect for the s.p.r.; but to subject either Sally or myself to their 'evidential' scrutiny is not my intention. The scentings were an inexpressible comfort, and just the sort of lovingly practical considerate thing she would think up to console me for her absence. When they began to fade I felt as bereft as a child feels when they take away the night light or some other comforter for the dark hours. Still, I understood that I must not expect that they should be kept up indefinitely, as a particular sign of grace and favour, however deep my sense of gratitude and blessing. In the end they faded; but even now, if I have been away for some time and come back late, a ghost of the same trail of flowery essences is apt to greet me evanescently, when I open the door.

Another mysterious thing during the first six months or so was the soft blue light, particularly in my bedroom. When I rested, as I often had to, in the day time, I seemed to be lying under the faintest, luminous blue mist, extraordinarily restful, like a healing colour bath. Around the window-frames and along the shelves beneath the windows it thickened and lay like a substance, as if an ethereal palette knife were spreading it. In the angle of the room, under the window, facing my bed, it gathered in amorphous clouds which I used to watch as if I expected (did I?) that out of this massed immaterial blue some spirit form might take shape and emerge.

6

Literally twenty-four hours after writing this last paragraph, I opened one of my 'bibles' – namely C. G. Jung's *Memories, Dreams, Reflections*, and re-read a passage which I had entirely forgotten. He is describing his unique experience in the ancient city of Ravenna, on the occasion of his second visit to the tomb of Galla Placidia.

'We went,' he says, 'directly from the tomb into the Baptistry. . . . Here, what struck me first was the mild blue light that filled the room; yet I did not wonder about this at all. I did not try to account for its source, and so the wonder of this light without any visible source did not trouble me.'

Neither did it trouble me. Blue is the colour of spiritual healing, though I did not know this at the time. Patrick was having the same experience of blue, and we several times mentioned it to one another as yet one more inexplicable blessing. Dr. Jung would, I presume, ascribe his perception of the mild blue light as a preparatory stage in that 'momentary new creation by the unconscious' by which he explains his vision of the 'four great mosaic frescoes of incredible beauty' which do not, in fact, exist . . . or no longer, in fact, exist. I am not an unquestioning disciple of this great man – one of the very

greatest of our century – and I do not always subscribe
to his interpretations in the field of the unconscious.
When it comes to interpretation, I cannot but be reminded of the story of the Devil walking one day with a
friend, and seeing somebody ahead of them stoop to pick
up something. 'What,' says the friend, 'did he pick up
just then?' 'He picked up a bit of the truth,' says the
Devil. 'Oh,' says his friend, 'is not this a sad day for
you?' 'Not at all,' says the Devil, with a chuckle, 'Wait,
just wait, . . . in a moment he will start to formulate it.'

I hope this does not sound arrogant, or cynical. The
important thing, for me, is that I saw (or think I saw!)
the same sort of diffusion of the blue ray that C. G. Jung
saw. Many others have seen it, of course, when endowed
with extended vision; and all spiritual healers, I believe,
make use of it.

Then there was the small miracle of my withering plant
that came to life again. I say 'miracle' because it was
not a matter of extra-sensory perception, not a subjective
matter. Somebody, some external agency, some invisible
Breath or Being must have been responsible for what
happened. It does not seem possible that my personal
thought-power can have had anything to do with it,
because, on that particular night, my thoughts were
frost-bitten-black enough, I should have thought, to blast
an oak tree.

It was about eight months after, and I came in late,
having been to a concert and supped afterwards. I
suppose the beauty of the music, in particular a certain

elegiac song, had brought Sally, and her absence, poignantly to mind. I sat on and on in my armchair, too inert even to make the effort to go to bed. I remember that that poem of Keats beginning: '*In a drear-nighted December, Too happy happy tree* . . .' slipped into my mind from nowhere and went on running through it. Beside me on a low table stood a small green plant which I had bought two or three weeks earlier. It had caught my eye among dozens of others more or less familiar to me in the florist's, because it was the only one of its kind, and its kind was quite unknown to me: the girl who sold it to me did not know its name. I was staring at it for some time in a semi-conscious way before becoming aware that it had collapsed: the tips of its feathery-spiny, vividly green fronds had all curled up like tiny paws. Yet I had not neglected to water it. To myself I said: 'Not even my plants . . . I can't even keep plants alive any more.' A hideous *accidie* – the kind of despair that breeds hell's climate – overwhelmed me. Surely other mothers have experienced the guilt and self-reproach I was unable to shake off at first. The dialogue runs roughly thus: Mother: 'My fault . . . was it my fault?' Child: 'You didn't keep me alive. Why didn't you?' Mother: 'Forgive me, I failed you. What did I do wrong? Did I fail there? . . . or there? . . .' *I must be wicked to deserve such pain* is the predominant burden.

Next moment, the little plant began lightly, very lightly, to quiver and tremble, as if the faintest possible breeze were brushing it. The shrivelled fronds shook themselves out, expanded, seemed to become energized. *Under my eyes* it grew, freshened, thickened out. I should think it grew a couple of inches as I watched; and became – as it remained to the end of its life – deliciously compact, vital, lustrous.

Not long after, I became nervously exhausted; and it was my good fortune to be sheltered by a practical saint if ever there was one – a widow with a pleasant country house near London. She had practised formerly as a masseuse and physiotherapist, and now received a few patients in need of . . . well, a breather; of rest, protection, of a hiding place, in the hope of avoiding total breakdown. I was there for a fortnight. My precious plant came with me; and when she visited me in bed that evening she noticed it at once. I asked her if she knew its name, and without hesitation she said: 'It's the Rose of Sharon. It's spiritually nourished.'

I don't know why she said this; because later when I was able to look up the Rose of Sharon in a botanical book it did not appear to be any relation to my plant; as she agreed.

This best and kindest of women died only two or three years later. She must have gone straight to heaven. My plant ceased to grow, but it remained glowing and vigorous, a midget burning bush, until I went to Greece for a holiday in the following June. Of course I left instructions that it should be tended; but when I came back three, weeks later, it was dead.

Years later, I discovered her mistake – Hugo found

for me another specimen of this strange plant: Rose of
Jericho, not Sharon. Its large dried-up brownish
rosettes blow about the desert. Put them in water and
they revive, turn green again and spread out little fronds.
However, my original plant remains an archetype.

7

It was within the first few months, but well after the
'great glimpse' I have recorded, that I was directed,
by the same friend, L., to two books by Geraldine Cummins: *The Road to Immortality* and *Beyond Human
Personality*. Everybody interested in the problems of
'communication' has studied the work of this dedicated,
utterly selfless explorer, shrewdest, most humorous and
delightful of human beings – miscalled an 'automatist'.
As she herself says in the preface to *Swan on a Black
Sea* – perhaps her most impressive contribution to the
field of psychical research – she would be more aptly
termed a recorder in writing of transmitted thought; and
it is this quality of intensely living, lucid, passionate
and personal thought which so struck me when I first
read these short, packed books that I felt in myself a
strong responsive vibration. It was as if an actual current
of spiritual energy were flowing to me from the pages;
as if I understood and were in harmony with the imagi-
natively creative nature of the alleged communicator,
F. W. H. Myers. In short, it was, for me, an experience of
picking up a bit of the truth; and I did not attempt to
interpret it: I just went on reading and re-reading; and

each time I did so, even at my flattest, the same sympathetic vibration kindled and sustained me. Everyone has
their first teacher in this or any other field, and he was
mine: whether or no every detail of the information he
imparted through Miss Cummins's hand is objectively
accurate is immaterial. Indubitably he had, and has
acquired, deep insight; but he is not omniscient. Before,
I had known him only as the author of that celebrated,
perfervid piece of writing, namely, his recollections of
George Eliot at her most sybylline and elevating, during
her visit to his Cambridge Courts. Later, of course, I
read his great pioneer research work, *Human Personality
and its Survival of Bodily Death.**

After this fortunate introduction to the subject I
went on unremittingly exploring it. My appetite for
psychic findings and experiences was insatiable: no
student can ever have raked the shelves of the library of
the College of Psychic Science more voraciously; none
can ever have received more help and kindness. My dis-
coveries thrilled and astounded me. I was being made
free of a vast, neglected, surely overwhelming body of
evidence of survival, associated with names of impeccable
integrity and intellectual eminence: classical scholars,

* I would like also to record my great debt to *The Imprisoned
Splendour* and other books by C. Raynor Johnson; to Jane Sherwood,
whose books *The Country Beyond* and *The Fourfold Vision* deeply
impressed me; to *The Silent Road* by W. Tudor Pole; also to Cynthia,
Lady Sandys, whose clairaudiently received scripts, soon to be
published) are at once the most 'human' and the profoundest, spiritually speaking, of any known to me.

poets, physicists, statesmen, philosophers. I had assumed, like most people – of course, like most people, without investigation – that communications from alleged discarnate entities were grotesquely, embarrassingly trivial; but, to my immense relief, I was presently able to see these in proportion, and though deploring disregard them, because of the immense amount of evidence for communication of a kind more intellectually and spiritually acceptable. Trying to discriminate, to sift the 'pure' from the 'coloured', to guard against such factors as pictures in the sitter's auric field or preconceptions, prejudices in the medium's personal subconscious, I became convinced – rightly or wrongly – that unimpeachably evidential records were available: these I absorbed until they became part of my thinking, feeling and breathing apparatus.

And all this that I was so avidly searching out and drinking in was not a modern discovery! – simply a contemporary, more scientific (and sometimes far less noble) restatement of truths known from the beginnings of recorded history. If modern atheists, or philosophical materialists, rejected them, relegated them to the realm of childish things outgrown, perhaps they were blinded by intellectual arrogance; perhaps they deliberately, perversely, chose to remain blinkered, not to inform themselves. The fact remained that the greatest of the world's great minds had always known, intuitively or suprasensibly, that we are souls travelling in eternity: the Tibetan and the Egyptian Books of the Dead, say it;

the Upanishads, the Bible, Socrates, Plato, Plotinus,
Shakespeare, Dante, Blake, Wordsworth, Keats, Shelley,
Emily Brontë, the Brownings, Tennyson, William James,
Rudolf Steiner, to name but a few . . . the list is inex-
haustible. Let me add to it the names of three profound
metaphysical thinkers, our contemporaries: J. G. Ben-
nett (*The Dramatic Universe*, Vol IV, particularly);
Douglas Fawcett whose difficult works *The Zermatt
Dialogues* and *The Oberland Dialogues* are scarcely known
as yet; and, of course, Teilhard de Chardin.

How strange now seemed the indifference of so many
to a subject of such paramount importance; how incomprehensible their suspicions or nervous or angry coldness,
their contemptuous mockery! Like dear F. W. H. Myers,
'I felt a knowledge almost greater than I could bear . . .
and yet a knowledge which none would receive from me,
an answer to which no one cared to listen, although the
riddle was at the heart of it all.'*

On the other hand, how sad, how disconcerting to find
the Great Question stained and smeared, not infre-
quently, with sectarianism, prima donna touchiness, hair-
splitting, back-biting, opinionatedness, and other forms of
unworthy behaviour, including the vilest of all – the sling-
ing of mud at the illustrious dead, their predecessors in
research.

I tried to remind myself that without first-hand
experience, I too might well have felt that I owed it to

* Ibid.

my integrity to remain sitting on the fence; or else given up, discouraged and embittered. I had embarked upon my researches *because of* an unassailable conviction; therefore I could not be acceptable to true-blue psychical researchers. They were austere scientific sceptics, and it was natural that they should regard me as a suspect case; cracked, credulous, unhinged by catastrophe. Had I confided to them my reasons for believing Sally to be still living and death not the end but simply a change of consciousness, their verdict of *non proven* would have chilled me even more depressingly perhaps than ridicule or bigoted disbelief.

So I remained lonely, secretly consoled, troubled, disorganized, intellectually engrossed, aggressively on the defensive. . . . And still without any true accretion of inner strength; still oscillating between tenuous exaltation and morbid dread; still, in spite of knowing that God, whatever God might be, had listened to me, that I had been granted these 'graces' because, for her sake, I had gone through death with her and would have done so gladly a hundred hundred times – still as far as ever from surrender; still in my pursuit of one loved being, one alone, self-separated from the source. I reminded myself of the importance of prayer and told myself I must, must really, learn to pray; but I felt self-conscious, I could not believe it would 'work'. Sometimes I wondered whether I should study some technique of meditation; but either the symbols interfered or I failed to concentrate, or in some other way I seemed to be prevented. I dared not consult priests or ministers of the Church for fear of hearing that Sally had gone to her Eternal Rest or had Seen God or was in Purgatory, or safe in the Everlasting Arms; and that I for my part must remember that the Lord giveth and the Lord taketh away and trust in His infinite mercy. Most of them would indeed have said so; but I know now what help and comfort I could have got from certain enlightened and erudite servants of the Church; but entrenched as I was in stubborn anti-clerical prejudice, I would not have believed it then. I feared above all that I would be told that it was sinful to attempt to communicate with the dead, and that if I continued in my wicked ways, God would see to it that I was cut off from Sally altogether. This threat was actually voiced by a well-meaning friend, a Roman Catholic convert, who exerted himself to draw me into the fold; he thought me stiff-necked and riddled with spiritual pride. However, it was through him that I met a delightful Jesuit Father who in the goodness of his heart used to pay me visits. I would have liked to go on seeing him; but I knew that I could never be an obedient daughter of his Church (or of any Church) and felt that I ought to cease to badger him with unanswerable questions. I envied the optimism of Christian Scientists, but could not accept Mrs. Baker Eddy's doctrines. I deeply admired the Quakers and would have felt happy in their silences; but I knew that their disciplines were not for me.

During that first year or so I dreamed often of being

back in early childhood. Nothing was changed from the
time when, like the child Dylan Thomas, I was young
and easy under the apple boughs. . . . Nothing was
changed, they were all there, though shadowy, and I
was just as I had once been, in the orchard, in the rose
garden, by the lily pond, beside the river, in the library;
or else, more than once, I was returned to that very spot
between laurels and silvered lawn where many years ago,
under the piercing moon, the world began to spin. From
these refreshing dreams I woke with a warm sense of
being cherished: I thought my parents were taking care
of me again, in the place where, the time when, we had
all been happiest. But now and then, without apparent
reason or conscious preparation on my part, my sombre
road was lit by dreams and visions of a different kind:
symbolic pictures, maybe, which ran through, yes,
through . . . though I could only grasp the edge of their
significance. Symbols reflecting my inner state? – or
glimpses of former lives? – Sometimes it seemed to me
that I was 'looking in' on moments of peak intensity,
always with a tragic undertone, in the history of my long,
long relationship with Sally.

One night I found myself wandering through a long
dark claustrophobic room. At first it seemed empty, but
then I saw that it was crammed, like a hospital ward,
with narrow, poor, iron bedsteads on which lay sick
people, shabby men and women, who watched me, not
with animosity, but with patient rather vacant faces; as

if, from lying too long inert, untended, loveless in this dismal place they had abandoned hope. Everything looked grubby and neglected; the walls were cracked and peeling. I thought with horror: 'I must get out of here, I know the way' – and I began to hurry round a corner which I knew would lead back into the garden of my childhood. But in the very instant of seeing my escape route open, I checked myself – or I was checked. I knew I must force myself to stay with these grey people, look at them, touch them, speak to them. Suddenly a bodiless voice said in my ear: 'Whom are you looking for?' – and I answered nervously: 'Well, actually for Sally.' Then the voice said: 'Don't you know she has been asleep for three days and nights?' On a current of inexpressible relief, as if saying to myself: 'So that's why I couldn't find her,' I went flying, with the voice beside me sweeping me up an invisible stairway and into a high vaulted upper room full of clear pale light, bare of furniture except for one plain simple carved wooden bedstead; and sitting up in this bed was Sally, all shining, in a dazzling white garment, with bare shoulders, holding her arms out and laughing to see my surprise and joy.

Another night I was standing at a roadside: it was an actual piece of landscape and I knew it well. The road I was watching was a rough dry sun-baked track, and opposite me was a broken sandy bank covered with green scrub grass and cactus, and topped with an umbrella pine. The picture was clearly defined, the colours glowing, natural. It might have been Crete, or some other part of

Greece? Or southern Spain, perhaps? I was watching
the road because I knew of some appalling danger that
was coming. All at once a troop of riders started to
approach me from the left, among them Sally and her
father. I saw them clearly though the rest were shadowy:
they were side by side, riding camels and looking boyish;
young soldiers, both of them, and carefree. In the same
instant, where the bank had been, a vision opened: a
golden bull, tiny and brilliant as if seen through the
wrong end of a telescope, head lowered, snorting, pawing
and trampling the dust with burnished golden hooves; like
a figure in the Zodiac come to life. Now the danger was
upon us, palpable: they were riding into it and I had to
save them. But it was coming from another quarter,
despite the bull's ferocious, charging stance: it was coming
from the right, where a bridge or parapet still hid what I
knew was about to show itself: the head of another golden
animal, but a huge one this time, with horns like a ram's
and a shaggy fleece. I cried out and woke in terror,
sweating, my heart hammering.

Lastly I must set down the 'dream' which has changed
my life, though not in any outward way. So high as I had
been lifted up, once, above my station, soon after Sally
left the earth, so low was I flung down that night,
flung to my knees, made to stare at my unwitting
arrogance, my blindness, my spiritual inadequacy; or
rather, to be shown that in the realm of spirit I was still
unborn.

I was asleep and dreaming horribly. A youth on a

bicycle, wearing a school cap. . . . The face (not a school-boy's in actual fact) was familiar, all too familiar, the expression cold, supercilious, smirking. He was watching me weep, examining my broken heart – an interesting specimen. There was some fear about my children in my mind. Then came a sort of thunderclap; a voice said loudly: *'Fall on your knees, be flung down'* – and with that I was hurled to the ground. I lay there extremely startled, wondering if I could have had a fit; if not, what force could conceivably have hurled me? I told myself this was absurd, I must get up, it really wouldn't do to stay prostrate on the floor like this. If I hadn't had a fit, or some frightful accident, I could obviously get up: I must put it to the test. (All this was happening of course to a "me" outside its body. My physical form was lying in bed asleep.)

I struggled to my knees. Then all at once, in front of me, the veils of darkness parted; strange light, like moonlight yet suffused with a coppery glow, illumined a scene suspended in mid-air. For a moment this scene was static: there was a kneeling figure in pale robes – a holy Being, obviously at prayer; in a landscape of rocks and desert. I thought: 'How very very odd. I must be looking at a painting by El Greco. . . . Some saint or . . .' Then the landscape became stereoscopic: I could see the ridges in the harsh baked earth, the mouldings in the rock surfaces. The figure was moving: still kneeling but leaning towards me as if – how to describe it? – as if encouraging me in my struggle to get up on my knees and rise. He extended his arms as if in a gesture, wide, slow, of inter-cession and looked at me intently.

I was made to look at him, for how long it is impossible to know. It seemed the face of a real person, though not one I had ever seen before. The beard was short and crisp, also the hair; the features were at once pronounced and delicate, the lips firmly modelled, with a full strong outline. The eyes . . . when I venture to speak of them, only one line seems adequate:

Stars, stars. And all eyes else dead coals . . .

Then I was awake, in the mid hour of a moonless night. Not a glimmer in the room. I had not been flung out of bed and hurled to the floor; yet I could still feel the shock of it, the difficulty of getting up. I thought madly of Paul on the road to Damascus, wondered if I could have been struck blind, switched the lamp on, read my watch, switched off again. In the dark, the dark face with its strange-coloured aureole of light seemed to go on quietly looking at me. I banished it. Did it even enter my mind, that night, that I was being tested, or, in no uncertain terms instructed? It did not. I did not get up, kneel down and pray. I was preoccupied with a surge of bitter disappointment. I was always hoping that Sally would show herself to me. Instead, a stranger, or Saint . . . or Someone . . . had shown himself – to me, of all people! Why? What could it mean! I was stunned.

Whoever it was could not be banished. Next day the scene came softly back: not itself, but the clear, weighing memory of it. *He came all so still.* . . . It was like that;

weighing on me, without weight, filling the empty spaces of my mind with a low-toned, irradiated image, an interceding gesture aimed at me, a look bent on me, silent, starry, attentive, day and night.

Was it an image of my own soul's making? Perhaps. I do not know. I cannot understand it. Sometimes I have told myself that it was the descent of some Being from the realms of Light, some Guide, or Elder Brother: one of those whose task it is to descend into dark planetary regions to rescue self-imprisoned souls. At other times I think, with awe, quite simply: 'You must believe it. You were looking at Jesus in the Garden of Gethsemane.' And if that is conceivable, then perhaps . . . perhaps I was permitted to recover some far-back knowledge lost or overlaid. Or else, since many are called, so we are told, could it have been some warning or 'alert'? Or else it is really true, what Jesus said: that He is with us always: available even to me, I dare to suppose, not because I sought for Him, but because of my seeking in the name of love.

At any rate, it was from thenceforth that I started to think about Him often, and to re-read the gospel accounts of what He said and did and ponder over them. Fascinating, exasperatingly sketchy and contradictory, disturbing documents; mystifying, uniquely vivid, revealed and hidden central figure, becoming real to me at last.

I began to see what it might be like to try to be a Christian. And it began to dawn upon me gradually – how gradually! – that that indifference, that nothing at the centre which I had imagined, was a misconception. We are not really bidden by our presiding angels to *go love without the help of anything on earth*. Help is available; although it does seem much too far out of reach for too many of us: or else, is it that we have willed that it should be so?

It seems fitting that this record, or testament, should write itself to an end in Sally's little house in the island. I lay down my pen and look out through the same long window to the spot where, nearly nine years ago, I saw the blackbird lying dead. Anna, to whom I dedicate this book, sits opposite me. For two days she has had her nose buried in a book, a Penguin, which has caused her recurrent collapses into quiet laughter. Now she has finished it and lays it down.

'A very sad book,' is all she says.

It is called *The Pursuit of Love*.

PART FOUR

LETTER TO ANNA

My dearest Anna,

I have long promised you that I would dedicate my next book to you: and here it is. Perhaps it's not quite the sort of book that you expected; but I hope you won't be disappointed. If you don't quite understand some of it now, one day you will. The only question that you will really feel like asking is: 'Is it a true story?' – and I promise you it is true.

This subject of life and death and of survival of death is terribly controversial, as you will discover; but I think you have had a better grounding than I had; and with a bit of luck you won't have so many set-backs. I believe, myself, that in another – well, perhaps fifty to a hundred years, it may well be *proved* that survival of death is a scientific fact; that the proof seekers will have proof of it, once and for all; but I also suspect that when it is there, at last, under their very eyes and ears, they will refuse to accept it. One of the things I have discovered is that many people have such a rigidly built-in resistance to the idea of 'going on', that nothing and no one will ever overcome it. So that if you imagine that you are bringing them tidings of comfort and joy by offering to share with them your own experiences,

141

or perhaps the enlightening books that you have read,
you will be in for a rude shock: you will be coldly
or nervously or contemptuously or even ferociously
repelled. You may be told in so many words – or if not,
it is all too easy to get the message – that, too weak to
keep a stiff upper lip, too undisciplined to 'assimilate
your grief' and carry on as usual, you have retired into a
world of tinsel and marshmallow fantasy. Apart from
their intellectual distaste – which is understandable
considering the amount of silliness, sensationalism,
vulgarity, credulity that muddies and clogs up the lower
reaches of spiritualism, fortune-telling, astrology and
the like – many people are violently prejudiced against
the notion of surviving death: even those (and I know a
few) who have had enjoyable and interesting and
privileged lives. 'It may be so, I suppose,' they say
grudgingly, 'but I don't fancy it. I don't want to hear
about it.' There is no answer to this! None of us wants
to dwell on distasteful subjects; and here I am reminded
of a story I read somewhere about F. W. H. Myers.
Finding himself alone one day in a railway carriage with
one fellow-traveller, he managed to steer the conversation
towards his favourite subject, namely the possibility of
our surviving death. But the stranger's replies became
ever more curt, exasperated and discouraging. However,
nothing daunted, Mr. Myers continued to press for a
straightforward answer: and finally received it. 'Well! –
we enter into the joy of the Lord, I suppose. But *why*
must we dwell on such unpleasant subjects?'

Nobody that I know, or that you know, is likely to frame such concepts in this day and age, let alone dwell on them with apprehension; but it is strange, incomprehensible, to me that the longing to be reunited with those whom we have loved is not universal. I had thought it unquenchable, eternal. But you might well get an answer such as this: '"Eternal" is a foolish, loaded word. Of course one never ceases to miss the dead to whom one has been attached. But they go on living in our memories – that is the only true immortality – until we too are snuffed out. And there's an end of missing, loving, longing.' I can't help feeling that in many cases this attitude is only skin deep, and represents a passionate protest against the seeming cruelties and frustrations of earth life. They imagine 'future life', 'eternal life' as a mere prolongation of this painful business. No wonder they don't fancy it.

But it was this pseudo-philosophical approach that most distressed me, I think, after Sally died: it made me feel . . . indignant is the word, I think. And what an emotional reaction it was thought to be! – to want her own continuing individual life for Sally: not a ghost life, subjective, dwindling, in our notoriously unreliable, enfeebled memories. Of course I realize that this reaction of mine is in itself no proof that what I wanted for her was what she would experience. All I wish to place on record is that, almost from the first moment of finding myself a mother without a daughter, the idea that such an exceptionally vital and richly endowed being as Sally should be suddenly reduced, in other people's minds, to such a sickly category, should be thus cut off from her actual identity – the idea seemed to me grotesque.

Perhaps, people will say, it was this passionate preconception of mine that induced my sub-conscious (useful portmanteau word!) to think up all the rest. The same sort of unaccountable preconception is supposed by many to have induced the writers and compilers of the gospels to think up Jesus as a man who once lived, historically, on earth. I imagine the fact is that, for some, the authentic ring, the vibration of reality is present in the Gospels; for others not. But still I wonder whom and what they think the Acts of the Apostles are about; not to mention the Epistles.

Now, a few words about psychism. People who have been, out of curiosity, to platform demonstrations of clairvoyance sometimes come away repelled and disillusioned. I don't wonder. But I do wonder why, after such an experience, they sometimes seem to consider themselves equipped to pronounce on the subject of mediumship and to dismiss it all as fraudulent rubbish. It is like calling yourself a specialist in music because you listen to a pop group (and by the way, always avoid using such words as 'rubbish', 'tripe' 'piffle', 'bunkum' about branches of knowledge you don't understand and don't intend to investigate. The words are horrid, coarse, infantile, and reflect badly on the user). I hardly ever watch public demonstrations of the psychic faculties nowadays, but I used to occasionally; and I was generally impressed by the integrity of the 'sensitive', even if sometimes the patter put me off. Now and then, such a startlingly evidential (if trivial) piece of evidence 'comes through' at these demonstrations that it starts the recipient on a voyage of exploration of his or her own; and that is the true value of the exercise, despite the melancholy fact that many seekers are content to remain at this elementary level and become 'message addicts'. Perhaps one shouldn't deplore anything that adds to people's happiness; but it does mean that the more progressive students and searchers are for ever battling against a heavy tide of inertia and sheer silliness.

The first time I ever attended a demonstration of clairvoyance was early in 1959, at the College of Psychic Science. My parents had been violently prejudiced against spiritualism (or what they had heard about it) and I really felt that I might be going to participate in an hour of moral shame and ethical dishonour. I persuaded my dear friend Peter, who died earlier this year, to accompany me: he looked very pale and shaky, and I discovered afterwards that he had been in mortal dread of getting a message from his father, with whom he had not always seen eye to eye. (He didn't! Even on an elementary level the law seems to operate: I mean the law of sympathy, of love.) I had heard that the demonstrator was a remarkable sensitive called Mrs. Ena Twigg. She is an attractive, charming-looking person, and I saw her with surprise and relief – having, I suppose, expected someone of the *Blithe Spirit* variety immortalized by Noël Coward and

Margaret Rutherford. In short, I began to relax. But what followed startled me tremendously. Mrs. Twigg whom I had never seen before opened her demonstration by addressing me. Then she described Sally, whom she appeared to see standing behind me; then she put her hands to her temples and said: 'This is a very strange message. . . . Why is she talking about the War God? She is saying Wotan, Wotan, the War God. . . . She is saying she does wish the War God would believe she is alive. . . . Can you understand?' Another pause. 'Oh! Now she's saying I haven't got the name quite right. It's not quite right but it's the only way she could think of to get it through. She is laughing. She says you will understand. Do you understand?'

Bearing in mind that your grandfather's name is Wogan you will see why Peter and I were both startled and impressed.

However, as I said earlier, this is deliberately not a 'psychic' book, simply a personal statement. I have had the good fortune to meet several marvellous sensitives, and they have become my friends, and given me great consolation, and changed the pattern of my thinking. I can never be grateful enough to them. All of them would say: sift and weigh for yourself, remembering always the tremendous difficulties and pitfalls inherent in attempted communication. I think too, that they would all say that physical mediumship as hitherto understood and practised belongs to a former age and should be abandoned. The aim should be, for each one of us, the raising of his

or her consciousness, to the point of achieving mental
and spiritual communion.

For my part I will go no further at present than to say
that I am convinced that it *is* possible to receive a good
deal of accurate and fascinating information about 'the
next world': that is, the more immaterial world inter-
penetrating this one, into which we shall pass when we
leave our physical bodies behind; also that I firmly
believe that it is important to try to learn as much about
it as possible before we slip quietly into it in our old age
or are thrust into it young, reluctant, unprepared, as, sad
to say, so many of the young, like Sally, are. They find
out later why for one reason or another they had to leave
the earth untimely; but at first it is often bitter for them.
One of the reasons why, in the early days, I felt certain
that I really was in touch with Sally was just that: I
mean, that she wasn't 'in bliss' or 'at rest' or anything
of that sort, but miserable, indignant and stubbornly
reluctant to accept the fact that her span on earth was
over. It was then that I was able to bring her help. I
believe that now she is experiencing modes of expanded
consciousness, intellectual and aesthetic, that she is
absorbed in various activities and services which language, as we know it, is inadequate to describe, although
her unusual powers of self-expression and her natural
strength of character and fine intelligence have enabled
her to seek out and establish lines of communication with
me which she values as deeply as I do. However, she
doesn't miss us as we miss her, because she is better able

to look in on our lives, particularly in times of crisis, joy or trouble.

Her new life sounds so rich and interesting that it is hard not to feel: 'I can hardly wait!' *But we have to earn these spiritualized and heightened modes of consciousness; we don't achieve them automatically;* and we must never forget the tremendous value and importance of our earth lives. We learn lessons here that can be learned nowhere else; and, after some trial and much error, I have realized that it is a great mistake to concentrate on 'hereafter' at the expense of here. We are all harnessed, or should be, to the needs of the age.

One impediment, very difficult to shift, is that 'only religious people believe this sort of stuff'. I think that if it could be grasped that we don't become bodiless wraiths, ghosts, shades or spirits when we die, but develop and inhabit a body if you like of finer matter, a subtle body, an astral or etheric body (these terms are interchangeable) – if this were grasped as true for all of us, whether or no we ever go to church, and true for all living things, sceptics might perhaps be less unwilling to suspend disbelief. Sensitives can see 'the dead' in their new bodies: I think it is possible that within the next (say) hundred years many more people will. Ordinary people like myself see and hear in flashes; and of course certain animals are much more finely equipped than humans with extended vision and hearing. These bodies are sometimes incredibly beautiful and self-luminous: not always: it depends. The sub-atomic worlds contain a myriad myriad forms, lovely, unlovely, strange, grotesque – and terrible.

I wish the Church would come out more positively and clearly on this important matter. After all, the Anglican Creed specifically declares belief in the resurrection of the body. In my rather lukewarm church-going teen-age days I found this article of faith so offensive to reason, feeling, and common sense that I used to press my lips firmly together while the passage was recited. Of course, it refers to the resurrection body, distinguished from the physical quite categorically by St. Paul. But nobody told me so. One was always left to infer that the only person who had ever risen from the dead was Jesus; and that the best we could hope for was that, 'through Jesus Christ', whatever that might mean, we might somehow achieve a feeble imitation of the same sort of transformation.

What humanity has said and done, all through the ages, in the name of *Credo quia impossibile est* never ceases to astound me; also what has been said and done, under the same banner, to poor humanity. Myself, I am by nature a person of little faith. Whenever I was told by well-wishers that all that was needed was one humble Act of Faith and lo! I should find myself safe and sound in the bosom of Mother Church, it seemed like being told that if only I would slip a pair of wings on I would find myself landing on the moon. So I am not unsympathetic to those who cry *Proof! Proof!* – though I always did understand, I think, that the mystical life can never be susceptible to the kind of proof which they require. Only direct experience can convince a doubter, once and for all: convince the doubter, that is, – not anybody else! Still, I have had the immense happiness of helping to convince several bereaved friends during these last years; or rather, I have been able to put them in the way of finding their own certainty. Others of course can't be approached; and on these one should never intrude.

Odd but true, you won't necessarily lead a more virtuous, more useful life because you believe that we 'go on'. You won't love the beauty of the world more, or appreciate the arts more deeply, or even love your fellow beings more and serve them better. You won't necessarily face death with greater equanimity. What I do think true is that you learn a greater sympathy with life in all its manifested forms of consciousness: for animals, birds, fish, trees, plants, as well as for human beings. Also, supposing that you were ever tempted to put an end to your own life you would refrain: not because it is a mortal sin that God will punish with damnation everlasting, as the cruel-minded old theologians used to teach, but because, generally speaking, it is a terrible *mistake*, a set-back that leads to bitter regret and self-reproach when those who have cut their own lives short wake up.

It is like being made free of an extra dimension; with, as I said, more respect for life in all its forms, more charity perhaps, and a much greater feeling of responsibility: because every moment can be thought of as a preparation. Also more patience; and more self-reliance when the time comes, as it does for most of us, sooner or later, when we have to face loneliness and come to terms with it. It is hard for you to believe (or isn't it?!) that when people grow old, particularly those who have to live alone, they spend a lot of time worrying about being a bore and a burden to the younger generation: perhaps finally becoming bedridden or senile or having to go into Old People's Homes. They would be happier if they had forward-looking thoughts inside them; and as a result quite possibly less of a nuisance, less apt to sink into melancholia, hopelessness; into physical and mental paralysis.

Sally was born with this innate sympathy for non-human as well as for human creatures. I have just been reading a letter which she wrote me from school at the age of eight. One sentence runs: 'I don't want Stephen Grubb to tea ever again thank you, because he is unkind to birds.' I forget the whole context of this declaration; but how characteristic is the 'thank you'! And vividly I remember an Easter at Llanstephan when she was perhaps eleven or twelve – I can't be sure. We had all gone down to the river to fish. It was a perfect April day, the birds calling rapturously, the banks of the Wye stippled and studded with budding branches, catkins, primroses. It was Sally's first lesson in the art of salmon fishing, and she was standing in the bows of the boat humming a tune (as usual) and casting quite stylishly, for a novice. I'm sure it had never crossed her mind that she might catch anything; but soon, to her stupefaction, her line tautened, tugged. Beginner's luck! . . . typical Sally luck.

. . . She was instructed and assisted, and did as she was told, with ever paler face and grimmer look. But when at last she actually saw the great form hooked, by her, gliding ever nearer to her just beneath the water, when the moment approached for the gaffing, she flung down her rod, leaped from the boat to the bank and stumped away, muttering over her shoulder: 'Somebody's blood for ever on my head.'

How she was teased and mocked when, that evening, she presented her plate for a helping of delicious salmon. 'None for Sally! She doesn't believe in catching fish, she thinks it's cruel.'

How taken aback, ashamed and bitterly upset she was. I suppose the lesson was a salutary one; but I couldn't help a sneaking sympathy with her unsporting instincts. In a story of mine called *Wonderful Holidays*, in which she figures as Jane, you will find recorded her similar feelings about sheep and calves 'who want their lives as much as we do. . . . I wish there wasn't *any* meat in the world. Meat, meat, nothing but meat. . . . I can't stand such a world.'

I have a fancy – call it only a fancy – that ardent sportsmen may be in for rude shocks in the hereafter. They might wake up in paradise – a paradise thronged with 'spirits of well-shot woodcock, partridge, snipe' (to quote from my favourite of all John Betjeman's poems) or with celestial deer-forests, or with bright streams and rivers chock-full of blessèd fish. But the creatures won't be for catching or for shooting. Immune from human weapons, they will be playing and going about their business; they will laugh to observe the frustration and bewilderment of their would-be killers; or, worse still, they will judge them. Imagine being looked at reproachfully by salmon, pheasants, otters, stags! . . . Perhaps, since each man loves the thing he kills (no irony intended) the next time one of these sportsmen came back to earth, he would choose to be a naturalist, or a, vet, or a game warden or some other kind of preserver of wild life. Someone might write a good book for children along these lines.

You were three and a half, Anna, when, between one week and the next, we had to give up your favourite game called *Packing to go to Java to see Sally*. Probably you have quite forgotten it. It was extraordinary how much you loved her and how much you missed her. Yet the first thing you said when the news was broken to you was: 'But Patrick will be alone.' For a long time after, whenever you came to tea, you insisted on visiting the sweet shop to buy him a bag of sweets 'because he can't buy them for himself.'

You were frequently my companion during those first months. Not having lost your 'early heart', you greatly enjoyed discussing death and graves and heaven; conjecturing Sally's whereabouts in the hereafter with a wealth of concrete detail. Some of your suggestions had a creepy flavour, like a child's in an Elizabethan play; some were bizarre in the extreme: I had to endure them for the sake of restoring to you Sally's shattered image.

'I wish Sally hadn't gone to heaven, why did she?' was a heart cry for more than a week, a month, more than a year. 'Nannie says it's because she was so good. Well I must say I hope I'm not too good, and I hope you're not. . . . I don't suppose you'll die for ages – not till I'm . . . oh! eighteen, I should think. I hope Mummy isn't all that good. She says certainly not. You're sure Sally got to heaven? *Some people sink down.* They rise up out of their graves but they can't open their eyes and they sink down. Are you absolutely certain Sally kept her eyes open?'

Another time you said suddenly: 'Sally's been dead so long now she's forgotten me. . . . How do you know she hasn't? She might be playing with another child. She might have got one of her own. I'll tell you something: people don't go to hospital in heaven. And another thing, in heaven, babies are born out of God's tummy. Did you know?'

And so on, and so forth, rattling on interminably. . . . But at least, with you, I could talk about Sally. People are apt to think one wants to lay one's dead on a shelf and lock the cupboard door. Some people *do* want that. They have such strange, shut-in, frightened thoughts about the dead. At least with you I could speak of living, not extinguished Sally.

I can remember when you were five, and staying with me in the Isle of Wight, I said, to tempt you to get to bed quickly:

'Your room is the one where people have the nicest

dreams.'

'Oh good!' you cried. 'Then I shall dream of Sally. Hurry, hurry.'

But you didn't dream of her, you told me suspiciously next morning. I'm not sure that you believed me when I explained that we often forget our dreams when we wake up.

Darling Anna, I'm afraid this isn't the book for children you used to badger me to write. But it *is* a book for children! And one day, if not now, you may like to read and think about it. Sally doesn't forget you, or any of us. How she might help you to put on your armour for the life before you, you must discover for yourself.

EPILOGUE

This is my last Testament.
What else is left that I might say?
I am in my eighty-first year, so
it seems more than likely that
this particular stage of my journey
is drawing to a close. Once, the
thought of living on through time
without fully seemed too huge, too
hopeless a burden to be borne; but
nowadays, I seem to live partly out of
time: so that that that lacerating
illusion we create by having to deal
life out in brackets of days, months,
years has largely disappeared.
Time past, time present, time future
are beginning to coalesce. I know
that eternity is not to come. We
are in it here and now.

EPILOGUE

Virago Press have invited me to add a chapter to this book, which first appeared in 1967. I am very grateful for the opportunity. As I write, the year 1981 is coming to an end. Re-reading these *Fragments*, I have found that I would like to add a few words: also that there are some alterations and corrections to the original text that I am anxious to make. One of these concerns a passage in my attempt at describing my first life-changing experience a fortnight after Sally's death. When she spoke of Patrick having to go on alone and of 'going to Auntie Peg', I interpreted it symbolically. But I learnt – from him – much later that he did in fact leave his flat that afternoon and, on an impulse, pay a visit to my sister Beatrix, in the hope of talking to someone close to Sally. So it seems likely that she was aware of this and giving me a piece of factual information. His career in the theatre was brief. Before long he found his true role, and is now well known as a poet, a novelist and a critic.

Far more to be regretted, because it now sounds to me insufferably patronizing and superficial, is the passage in which I declare myself a 'not unquestioning disciple' of C. J. Jung. The exigencies of re-printing prevent me from altering the text itself; so the best I can do is to say now that I am still too ignorant to class myself as any kind of a disciple of this outstanding genius. I am simply one of the multitudes in-debted to a man who was surely one of the greatest bene-factors to humanity of this century.

I do, however, sometimes find his language (in translation) dense and heavy going; and some of his interpretations of psychic phenomena difficult to accept – or rather, to under-stand. The point of genuine interest remains: it would appear that I saw the same diffusion of the blue ray that Dr Jung saw. I am told by sensitives that it is a potent factor in spiritual healing.

Anna, to whom I dedicated *The Swan in the Evening*, is now a wife and mother. My other four late joys, Guy, Roland, Kate and Ivo, are near the verge of adulthood. So in some respects my *Letter to Anna* is obviously out of date. However, I cannot change it much – I do not really want to. I hope it does not sound didactic, as one (private) critic wrote. It was an attempt to say something I had learned about life after death in a way a child might understand. And this is still Anna's book. The relationship with Sally that became evident while she was still a baby has remained 'something far more deeply interfused' than can be rationally accounted for. We shall know more one day.

I note that the same 1967 critic finds 'a profound inhibition lurking somewhere' (lurking? – how menacing it sounds!) which 'drags against my intention'. If this is at all true, it must have stemmed from a not unnatural hesitancy, a fear of sounding dogmatic or over-assertive; above all, of exposing Sally to derision, cynicism, scepticism.

It seems odd, with hindsight, that so many readers in the sixties – even the hostile ones – remarked on my *courage*. Perhaps, considering the climate of those times, it was courageous, or maybe reckless, to testify to my personal discovery that death does not extinguish life. But the climate has changed rapidly during the last twenty-five or thirty years. Matter has disappeared. Energy is now the key word. The nature of the universe itself, the probability of multiple universes, of infinite co-existent dimensions of space/time, all aspects of the paranormal, once unorthodox or unmentionable, are now open to discussion among physicists, psychologists – even biologists.

The pattern of this book took shape after I had told Laurens van der Post that I had got to write it and couldn't see its shape. Something he suggested about dividing it into three youth-times – my own, Sally's, Anna's – triggered off one of those unaccountable inner flashes: presently, the words began almost to write themselves.

I was alone in the Isle of Wight on the day of publication; my rigidly suppressed anxieties were beginning to nibble at me. Ignored? . . . Of course ignored . . . Held up to ridicule, contempt? . . . With the *Sunday Times* and the *Observer* under

my arm, I wandered along the Turf Walk till I found an un-
occupied bench, sat down and said to myself: NOW. Presently, familiar names were swimming giddily before my eyes
– Cyril Connolly Rosamond Lehmann Philip Toynbee Rosamond Lehmann . . . I think I literally passed out for a few
moments; then, trembling uncontrollably, I forced myself to
concentrate.

Shall I ever forget the relief, joy, gratitude that flooded
through me as I took in the sympathy and respect with which
these two influential critics treated Sally and myself?

After that bonus, I was able to confront other notices without too much loss of equilibrium; but, today, re-reading them
and also the many letters that reached me, has been an upset-
ting experience. They were mostly very sympathetic; a few
were nervous, dubious; one or two have revived perhaps
unjustified annoyance. Whatever their contents, they were
bound to uncover poignant memories. But, more important,
thanks to Virago, I have the good fortune to be able to take up
a few points of importance to myself and to clarify or empha-
sise them.

The term 'spiritualist' is still used opprobiously in orthodox
religious or agnostic intellectual circles. It is generally based
on that contempt prior to investigation which Herbert
Spencer defined and deplored more than a hundred years ago;
still, I can understand that an aura of cheap emotionalism and
charlatanism still clings to it. I object to the label chiefly
because I object to all divisive labels; they are apt to lead to a
narrowing of spiritual perspective, to dogmatism or parochi-
alism. Sects, cults, 'isms' of all kinds seem more flourishing
today than ever; but I am by nature a non-joiner, and –
figuratively speaking – I don't want to enter anybody's
ashram. I am no more specifically attached to spiritualism
than I am to theosophy or anthroposophy or Christian
Science, though I respect and have learnt from all these fields
of exploration. Anyone who takes the trouble to enquire into
the activities of the College of Psychic Studies (of which I am
one of the Vice-Presidents) or to read its quarterly journal,
Light, will know the breadth and quality of its work in various

scientific and psychological fields, apart from those loosely covered by the terms paranormal, mystical, metaphysical, esoteric.

One critic wrote (privately) with distaste of 'descriptions of mediumistic séances which you have obviously come deeply to doubt'. I cannot spot anything in my text that might give that impression; and 'séance' is another loaded word which I avoid because of its accretions of vulgarity and jokeyness; but the work of sensitives, their development and training, remains of deep interest and concern to me; and my debt – not only mine – to certain selfless, dedicated, wonderfully gifted sensitives is immeasurable.

I have just rediscovered a long review by Stevie Smith, written in 1968. For her my book 'opened a world of anarchy . . . Miss Lehmann says that Sally came back from the grave laughing and happy in a spiritual body'; and further on:

> Surely of all the theories of life after death the Christian – Judaic ones are the most comforting. The souls of the departed are in the hands of God and no harm can touch them. Nor can we help but feel that among the harms that might touch them were they not protected by God (or by non-existence if you are an atheist) is the harm of earthly lovers trying to get in touch with them . . . Miss Lehmann thinks that people who do not wish to traffic with the dead are cold, careless or timid. They may be more full of love than she thinks. For if you believe in God you will let the dying go, glad that the pain of loss is ours, not theirs. Is it asking too much that we should love our dead and leave them alone, waiting for our own deaths to know what it is all about? Or to know nothing ever again.'

I remember that this notice, with its raw note of censure, hurt me, particularly coming from Stevie whom I thought of as a friend – although very rarely seen – and as an admired colleague. What in the way of protest or argument I sent her I have forgotten. Here is her reply.

Dear Rosamond,
Thank you very much for your letter, I am only sorry my review seemed to you hostile. To the idea of life after death I found in your book, and which I perhaps too loosely described as spiritualism, I

am hostile; but not to you. I hoped I had made this clear, and also made clear how much I admired your courage and the beauty of much that you have to say, and the way you say it...

Some wretched nerve, you may say, has been touched. And this is true. I do not see the dead as a 'frightening and hostile society', but as being...either non-existent, or, in the hands of a loving God. All else seems to me anarchy, with the attendant dangers of dream upon dream and heaven (or perhaps not heaven) knows what of the unrecognised and unwished for coming in. I love the thought of 'departing' and of the human pattern being broken for ever, either in nothingness or in love that is beyond our thought. I did not use 'traffic' as a sneer, far from it. I was thinking of Pater's 'trafficked for strange webs with Eastern merchants', I expect. The webs may be stranger than we think, but the harm will be to us, I am sure we cannot touch the dead. All of which goes to show how right you are when you so gently imply (quoting my *Guardian* poem – which appears, without my knowledge, to have wandered into *The Christian Agnostic*) how very imperfect an agnostic I am. I love to think of the dead as in the hands of God and safe from us. So there we are, both of us, I expect, so far as here and now goes, in the hands of our temperaments.
Love from,
Stevie

The poem I must have quoted to her was the one beginning:

> *Oh Christianity, Christianity*
> *Why do you not answer our difficulties?*
> *If He was God He was not like us,*
> *He could not lose.*
> *. . .*
> *Oh what do you mean, what do you mean?*
> *You never answer our questions.*

This cry of exasperation and distress has always had a strong appeal for me. As Stevie said, it was quoted in his admirable collection *The Christian Agnostic* by Dr Leslie Weatherhead (who once wrote me a much prized letter about my book). Stevie would have agreed, I think, with Dr Weatherhead, who wrote in his introduction: 'If Christ came back in the flesh, He might say: "My house shall be called the house of reality, where men find the True God, but some of you have made it a

163

den of superstition and a stage for bewildering charades."

I don't know what True God, if any, Stevie ever found; but I have recently been reading her Lecture to the St Anne's Society entitled 'Some Impediments to Christian Commitment' published in *Me Again*, her 'Uncollected Writings' (Virago Press, 1981), and I cannot imagine a more impassioned Apologia for agnosticism – that is, with regard to the blood-stained history, the dogmas and doctrines of the Christian Church. To be able to write it, she must have pondered very deeply and seriously and come to many of the same conclusions as myself about certain of those 'tenets of Christianity' invented and consolidated by blinkered theologians throughout the ages.

In another essay she wrote:

> if one is tired all the time, I do not see how one can accept the Christian religion that is so exhausting, and tied up neatly for all eternity with rewards and punishments and plodding on (that too much bears the mark of our humanity with its intolerable urge to boss, confine and intimidate.) . . . one wants the idea of Death, you know, as something large and unknowable . . . Or perhaps what one wants is simply a release from sensation, from all consciousness for ever.

Perhaps she found in my book that tendency to 'boss and confine' which she so much disliked; and she may well have imagined 'the next world' as a glum pedestrian extension of the present one. If so, no wonder she didn't fancy living on. No wonder, too, that she plays with a romantic conception of Death as friend, almost as dream-lover, haunting her poetry under a uniquely memorable guise.

She had, I suspect, no taste for mysticism; and it would appear that despite her forceful onslaught, she and the tenets still clung to one another, nostalgically, and as a safeguard against 'anarchy'.

As for that harsh review, and her disarming letter, they seem to me muddled and somewhat contradictory statements, on the one hand, revealing a rejection of humanity, a longing to be done with Earth and 'earthly lovers': how otherwise could she see them as harming the dead they love? On the other hand, she sports with Death rather as a child does, surrounding the magical dread figure with sweet dreams and fantasies.

Perhaps – who knows? – there is wisdom buried in these ambivalences. Myself I was obliged not to remain playing and dreaming. I had no option but to be confronted with reality. I did not describe Sally as 'laughing and happy' in the first days after her departure. Quite the contrary: confused, incredulous, passionately resentful, desperate to reach me for reassurance – hers as well as mine. The young who go over unprepared, as she did, are not happy. The pain of loss *is* theirs, different from ours perhaps but as agonising at first as ours. To 'leave them alone' is to my mind truly 'cold careless and timid', although I realise that it is an attitude based on that old bogey of superstition – fear of 'holding them back', of disturbing what the Church offers them: eternal rest.

The last letter I would like to quote from came from William Plomer, fine poet and novelist, dear friend, much missed, of many years.

'I have read the book carefully', he says,

> and feel that anything I can say can perhaps only be what you already know . . . You have been candid about your most personal feelings and have therefore taken the risk – the calculated risk – of being read by unsympathetic readers. You have made no concession to intellectual bigots, agnostics, "humanists" and glib rationalists who think they know everything and don't allow either for their own fallibility or for what is mysterious or inexplicable. (I don't myself use words like supra-normal or supernatural as a rule because I can't feel that phenomena so designated are detached or apart from "ordinary" life.) [cf. Rilke's similar statement on the same theme which I have quoted earlier!]

William goes on to describe his first experience of bereavement at the age of four,

> when my Mother had to hold my second brother in her arms in a hovel in the Tropics while his throat was cut (it was called tracheotomy) by an incompetent doctor. I clearly remember the heat, the full moon, the sound of weeping. Her loss put a great strain on her beliefs but did not destroy them. To you I think Christianity does

not offer sustenance...Dearest Rosamond, I have learnt from this, the most personal of your books, how you were able to find your own separation from the most lovable of daughters not final separation.

In my reply I assured him that Christianity, or at least that glimpse of its Mysteries which my vision had disclosed to me, now meant *everything* to me. He wrote back saying that he supposed he had meant the Church of England, which he loved because its traditions, its tolerance and broadmindedness made room, he felt, for all who come. Again, we are in the hands of our temperaments I suppose. William's was religious. I don't exactly know into what category I would fall. I love the Anglican Church seen through the novels of Trollope, say, or Barbara Pym or through that masterpiece by Pamela Hansford Johnson, *The Humbler Creation*; but I am still a heretic and likely to remain one. Still, those eyes, that gesture of my vision are constantly before my inward eye; they give me hope that I shall never again fall out of love's true circle.

I believe that the four gospels, which so often read to me like code messages, tantalisingly cryptic, sometimes disconcerting, *(oh what do you mean, what do you mean?)* are only just beginning to be deciphered; and that the meaning of the life of Jesus on earth is of supreme importance to man's wholeness.

People who have read my book quite often write to me or ask to come and see me—mostly bereaved mothers. Their extraordinary dignity in affliction is infinitely moving; and I have learnt how ineluctably personal to each individual bereavement is. I am not a teacher; and 'counselling' is too grand a name for the help I try to give. I have come to feel that the best I can do is to *listen*: listen with a totally self-obliterating measure of attention. Sooner or later a kind of telepathic situation becomes established—not with me as a person but with a sense of Presence, delicate but unmistakable: a breath of spiritual fragrance steals in, quickening the air; a shimmer of energy, to borrow a lovely phrase of Cyril Connolly's. And presently all tension is dissolved. The tears that fall flow from a far less leaden source. Speech starts to come easily, without need for apology or for 'trying to be brave'. By some mysterious agency the great spiritual paradox discloses itself and can never be forgotten: I mean, that our starkest solitude is in reality accompanied, that there is peace, love, even moments now and then of purest joy deep down in the order of things as they truly are; and that this will be found at last, no matter how long the intolerable journey each one of us must take.

I have learnt to be careful about recommending the literature that I myself have found consoling or illuminating: it may fail to resonate or ignite for others. Or else they do not share my voracious appetite for the excellent literature that is available. By the same token one learns that for some, a little 'counselling' goes a long way. After the initial heart-cry, some prefer to seal the lid on further exploration: as if these were heavy luggage to be sent on ahead and collected later at some inexplicit future destination. I now realize better than I used to how understandable this is. Again, I am sometimes asked if I always recommend sitting with a sensitive. The answer is no – only when I am asked for my opinion, and whether I know whom to suggest then I gladly go into the whole subject to the best of my ability.

This is my last testament. What else is left that I might say? I am in my eighty-first year, so it seems more than likely that this particular stage of my journey is drawing to a close. Once the thought of living on through time without Sally was too huge, too hopeless a burden to be borne; but nowadays I seem to live partly out of time: so that that lacerating illusion we create by having to deal life out in packets of days, months, years has largely disappeared.

Time past, time present, time future are beginning to coalesce. I know that eternity is not to come: that we are in it here and now.

Over the years I have been taught by Sally and by others, some of them discarnate, something of how it will be when I wake up after I have shed my body; so I look forward, I look forward. But physical bodies fight so tenaciously sometimes to hang on. I do pray that mine will let go easily. No matter how far ahead of me Sally has gone – and I know she has – she will be waiting, as she promised. She will pull me through the door.